"Look, I'm not taking no for an answer," Slade said to her. *"I want to give this baby a name."*

"The baby *will* have one," she said through clenched teeth. "Mine."

"I want to marry you, Sheila. I want to marry you before the baby's born."

It was now or never!

Dear Reader,

What a month of wonderful reading Romance has for you! Our FABULOUS FATHERS title, *Most Wanted Dad,* continues Arlene James's miniseries THIS SIDE OF HEAVEN. Single dad and police officer Evans Kincaid can't quite handle his daughter's wild makeup and hairdos. Luckily—or not so luckily—the pretty lady next door is full of advice....

Do You Take This Child? is the last book of Marie Ferrarella's THE BABY OF THE MONTH CLUB miniseries—and our BUNDLES OF JOY title. Any-minute-mom-to-be Dr. Sheila Pollack expects to raise her baby all alone. But when the *long-absent* dad-to-be suddenly bursts into the delivery room, Sheila says "I do" between huffs and puffs!

In *Reilly's Bride* by Patricia Thayer, Jenny Murdock moves to Last Hope, Wyoming, to escape becoming a bride. But the town's crawling with eligible bachelors who want wives. So why isn't she happy when she falls for the one man who doesn't want to walk down the aisle?

Carla Cassidy continues THE BAKER BROOD miniseries with *Mom in the Making.* Single dad Russ Blackburn's little son chases away every woman who comes near his dad. It just figures the boy would like Bonnie Baker—a woman without a shred of mother material in her!

And don't miss the handsome drifter who becomes a woman's birthday present in Lauryn Chandler's *Her Very Own Husband,* or the two adorable kids who want their parents together in Robin Nicholas's *Wrangler's Wedding.*

Enjoy!

Melissa Senate,
Senior Editor

Please address questions and book requests to:
Silhouette Reader Service
U.S.: 3010 Walden Ave., P.O. Box 1325, Buffalo, NY 14269
Canadian: P.O. Box 609, Fort Erie, Ont. L2A 5X3

MARIE FERRARELLA

DO YOU TAKE THIS CHILD?

ROMANCE™

Published by Silhouette Books

America's Publisher of Contemporary Romance

To
Mary Theresa Hussey and Debra Robertson
for wading through all this
and keeping the sequence straight.
Thank you.
(Wasn't it fun?)

 SILHOUETTE BOOKS

ISBN 0-373-19145-6

DO YOU TAKE THIS CHILD?

Copyright © 1996 by Marie Rydzynski-Ferrarella

Printed in U.S.A.

MARIE FERRARELLA

lives in Southern California. She describes herself as the tired mother of two overenergetic children and the contented wife of one wonderful man. She is thrilled to be following her dream of writing full-time.

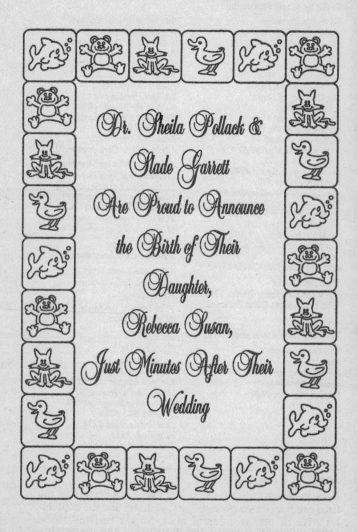

Dr. Sheila Pollack & Slade Garrett Are Proud to Announce the Birth of Their Daughter, Rebecca Susan, Just Minutes After Their Wedding

Chapter One

Slade Garrett stretched within the limited confines of his car and stared out at the tall glass-and-concrete medical building standing at the end of the parking lot. The numerous panes of the eight-story structure caught the afternoon sun, turning the rays to rainbows in flight.

He squinted as he stared, but he didn't get out. And he didn't leave.

Slade passed his hand over his face. It was the first time he'd shaved in more than two months. He kind of missed the beard. Grooming hadn't seemed very important these last few months, not where he'd been. But he had stopped to shower and shave before boarding the transatlantic flight that had ultimately brought him here.

Damn fool idea, coming here.

But it had been an idea that had sustained him for the last—what? Nine months? At least. It had ridden shotgun with him like a silent partner, a specter unaffected by the atrocities that he had routinely recorded on his beat. A beat that included parts of the world that the readership of his newspaper would just as soon forget existed once their fascination with the horrific events ended.

At times he had felt as if he'd been trapped within the confines of a bad movie, except that it hadn't ended in two hours and there was no one to yell "cut" and make it stop.

It was then that thinking about coming back, about seeing Sheila again, about running his hands along her cool, long limbs and breathing in the rare scent along her neck, had kept him going. It had kept him sane. She more than anything else had been urging him on to the end of the goal line.

A goal line that he himself had kept moving farther and farther along every time he extended his assignment, every time he agreed to be sent to somewhere else where people no longer had a bed to sleep in, or enough food to keep their bellies from rumbling and tightening by the end of the day.

It was his job and he'd loved it once, loved the excitement. But now he wasn't so sure anymore. Wasn't sure of anything except that he had to see her just one more time.

So now he was here. And he wasn't moving. Not forward, not back.

Restless, edgy, Slade reached to his breast pocket, then muttered under his breath. Funny how even after five months, it still surprised him not to find anything there. Funnier still to pick the middle of a "conflict," so named because it was too small to be called a war, to decide to give up cigarettes. Smoking had been a bear of a habit to kick.

But he had done it because he didn't like being a slave to anything: habits, urges, or people. The only thing that Slade adhered to with any amount of faithfulness was his own code of ethics.

Beyond that, he wanted nothing to lay claim to him. When he found himself reaching for a cigarette before his eyes were focused, he knew it was time to stop. He refused to be imprisoned by a craving.

So what the hell was he doing here, sitting in a car, staring at a building where she was supposed to be, half an hour after he'd turned in his latest series of articles to his editor's assistant?

Proving to himself that a dream didn't have a hold on him, either.

Or so he hoped.

It wouldn't have a hold on him, he argued, not once he saw that the dream was only that, just a dream. A mirage given mythical proportions because of time and distance. And circumstances.

If he'd seen her more than just for that one magnificent evening, if she had been part of his life on a regular basis, she'd be history now. Just like all the other women who had passed through his life were, instead of this vision he'd carried around inside his head.

A vision he wasn't certain he really wanted to relinquish. And yet, to be who and what he was, he had to.

Slade rolled down his window and took a deep breath. Carefully manicured bushes at either sides of the lot released the fragrance of the white blossoms they briefly housed.

April in Southern California.

He'd forgotten what that felt like. The weather was more refined here, only on occasion interfering with little things, like picnics on the beach or camping trips. There was no life-and-death threat of monsoons that could wipe away a lifetime of scrambling in less than a blink of an eye.

Yes, he reminded himself, his mouth curving with a touch of cynicism, *but we have earthquakes.*

Somehow, it just wasn't the same. It didn't balance things out. The image of incredible, soul-wrenching poverty had been indelibly inscribed on his brain.

Slowly, the song on the radio penetrated his thoughts, refocusing them. Johnny Mathis was softly singing about a date never quite reached on the calendar. Slade's smile softened.

The orchestra had been playing a Mathis melody the night he met her, Slade remembered. He closed his eyes, letting the song waft over him. He could almost see her now, standing there across the room, surrounded by a battalion of people, and yet, she might as well have been alone for all the difference the others made to him.

He saw only her....

She caught his eyes almost as soon as he walked in. The woman with the striking, classic profile was the most beautiful woman he had ever seen, Slade thought as he observed her across the crowded banquet room.

He fingered the stem of his wineglass, no longer tasting his drink. Watching her, he almost forgot how much he hated wearing formal clothing that had been designed with mannequins in mind.

Watching her, he'd almost forgotten everything else, as well.

Leaning over, he'd asked the closest person to him, an older lady with the face of a pixie, "Who is that woman?" He raised his glass toward the woman in question. "That tall blonde with the circle of men around her." A circle of men he intended to extricate her from.

The woman tilted her head as she appraised him, obviously attempting to ascertain who he was. Her manner indicated that he should have known the answer.

"That's Dr. Sheila Pollack. She's on staff with the hospital. Her parents are Doctors Susan and Theodore Pollack. They're sponsoring the fund-raiser for Harris Memorial's new obstetrics wing."

She'd said something further to him, something about what was printed on his invitation. But it was lost in the sea of background noise as Slade forged his way over toward the tall, willowy blonde in the royal blue evening dress.

The dress sparkled almost as much as she did, and came down to somewhere along the middle of her thigh, resting comfortably in a place that he would have found infinitely stimulating were he in the same area.

He could feel his excitement growing as he approached her. It was the same exhilarating feeling he experienced whenever he found himself closing in on a story. He enjoyed the challenge of unraveling mysteries, and she had the air of a good page-turning thriller.

"Hi, I'm told that you're involved with this fund-raiser."

Sheila turned away from the man she was talking with to look at him. Her eyes were huge and blue, like cornflowers in the spring. Slade found that proximity did not diminish the impression she cast. It reinforced it.

"I'll talk to you later," the man mumbled, moving away from her. He melded into the crowd, disappearing before his absence was even noticed. An alley cat giving way to a lion.

Sheila slowly looked Slade over. He didn't appear familiar. He couldn't be one of her patients' husbands. She would *definitely* have remembered someone who looked like him. Smiling, she asked, "Have we met?"

"No, but that's easily remedied."

Very efficiently, with a minimum of movement, he slipped his arm around her shoulders and cut her off from the circle she'd been in. Slade eased her over to the side. The terrace doors opened at their back, displaying an array of stars on a blanket of black velvet.

"We both know that lady in beige over there." He nodded vaguely toward where he had been standing a few moments ago.

Sheila looked over to where he indicated. "You mean Martha?"

He nodded agreeably. She was wearing some kind of scent that fired his blood. He wondered if she was involved with someone and if that mattered to her. It didn't to him. Not at this moment.

"Yes, Martha."

It felt as if his eyes were touching her all over. Sheila felt herself growing warm. With effort, she retained the humor in her eyes. "And what if I told you that her name isn't Martha? That it's really Jane?"

"Then I'd say that you'd had a lapse of memory, as did I. It isn't Martha, or Jane." He studied Sheila's eyes and knew he'd guessed correctly. A grin that was meant to disarm her flashed across his face. "Am I right?"

Sheila took an instant liking to him. Delighted by his answer, she laughed. "Yes, you're right. It's Sibyl. Her name," she prompted in case he thought she was introducing herself. She put out her hand to him. "Sheila Pollack."

Slade shifted his drink to his other hand. "Yes, I know. I'm with the *Times*."

He saw her eyes take quick measure of him, as if she was accustomed to assessing people.

The only people from the *Times* were those who were writing this up in the society section. "You don't look like the typical society columnist that the paper sends."

Which was a relief, he thought. Not that he had anything against gossip. Like everything else, it had its place in the scheme of things and helped sell papers. But he didn't place gossip columnists in the same league as real reporters. The underbelly of life that they dug up didn't begin to compare with what he dealt with on a regular basis.

He also realized that it meant she was accustomed to attending these sorts of affairs. Or throwing them.

"Very astute." He raised his glass in a mock salute. "I'm not. But Laura Moore became ill at the last minute, so here I am."

He'd done it on a whim, as a personal favor to a woman he'd once been intimate with. Funny where a whim could lead you, he thought, savoring the sight of the regal woman beside him.

Slade took another sip of his drink. "Remind me to send her flowers."

Intrigued, she asked, "Why?"

A waiter meandered by them, holding a half-empty tray aloft. Slade depleted it by one more as he took a glass of white wine and handed it to Sheila. She inclined her head in silent thanks as she accepted it.

"Because," he explained, "if she hadn't gotten sick, I never would have gotten to spend the evening with you."

Sheila smiled above the rim of her glass, her eyes teasing his. The man moved slowly only compared to a Concorde jet. "You haven't yet."

No, but he would. He could feel it. His mouth quirked in a smile as he looked into her eyes. She was daring him to make it a reality.

"Oh, but we have Martha-Jane-Sibyl between us." She began to turn away. He talked faster. "That makes us almost old friends." Because it felt right, he slipped his free arm around her shoulders again, and this time he kept it there. "Wouldn't you want to keep an old friend company on his last night in the States?"

She wondered how many stories he was capable of if put to the test. "Shipping out? What, are you a sailor as well?"

The word *sailor* created an instant fantasy in his mind. He was a pirate and she the noblewoman he'd kidnapped on the high seas. He wondered which of them would beg for mercy by the end of the night.

"No, but I really am a reporter, a foreign correspondent, and I've got an overseas assignment. I leave tomorrow morning."

Sheila wondered if he was just spinning a story for her benefit, or if he was telling the truth. She could picture him as a foreign correspondent. There was something roughly exciting about him, despite the classy lines of his tuxedo.

"London?" she guessed.

It would undoubtedly be safer there, but he probably would have been bored to tears. Slade shook his head. "Bosnia."

The answer surprised her. She thought of the stories on the nightly news and tried not to shiver. "If you're saying that for effect, you've succeeded."

"Good."

He toyed with a wisp of hair at her nape. It curled in the opposite direction than the other tendrils that were cascading around her head. A rebel, he mused. Was she one, too? He watched her eyes as they grew just a shade larger.

"But it's true, nonetheless. I'm not here as my editor's first choice to cover an assignment—"

She laughed. "Big surprise." She sipped from her glass.

He began to wonder what it would be like to have those lips touch his, what it would be like to make slow, passionate love to her.

"I'm here as a favor," he continued casually. "Laura needed someone to take notes for her." He smiled as he thought of how he'd given in and what Laura had said as he'd hung up. "She thought after tonight, I might welcome the overseas assignment." He decided, by the way the dress adhered to Sheila's body, that she was wearing very little beneath those sparkling sequins. He also decided that he wanted to verify his theory firsthand. "I was going to agree with her—"

Sheila lifted her chin, amusement dimpling her mouth. "Until now?"

His eyes touched hers and they both laughed silently. "Yes."

She took another sip before commenting. "Laying it on with a shovel, are we?"

He took no offense. He liked a woman confident enough not to need flattery. "Too much?"

She inclined her head, her eyes laughing at him. "Just a tad."

He wanted to get to know her better. Wanted to spend the evening with her and knew he had to act quickly before she slipped away from him. There were more than enough men around to take her away. He'd have to be blind not to notice the way they were looking at her. The way, he knew, he was looking at her.

Slade smiled engagingly. "Want to start over?"

She smiled in return, really smiled, and it reminded him of sunrises he'd seen as a kid in Missouri. "Sure, why not?" She put out her hand. "Hello, I'm Dr. Sheila Pollack."

He shook her hand and held it in his a moment longer than was necessary. They both liked the contact. "And I have a pain." With a dramatic flourish, he placed his other hand over his heart. "Right here."

Very gently, she eased her hand from his. "Funny." Her eyes shone with amusement. "I would have diagnosed the pain as being a little lower than that."

"I like you, Dr. Sheila Pollack."

And he did. For him, it was always that fast. He wasn't the type to mull things over and examine them beneath a microscope. A thing was either right, or it wasn't. And Sheila Pollack was right. Right for him, right for this moment in time within his life.

The warmth of her smile told him that the feeling was mutual. "I already gathered that."

Pretending that they were still in the introductory state, he continued, "Don't you want to know what my name is?"

Her eyes told him that she already had a name for him. He wondered if it was flattering. "I'd rather see your press card. At least then I'd be convinced that some of this story is true."

Vibrant but cautious. An interesting combination. He rather liked that.

When he handed her his wallet, opened to the press card, Sheila actually looked surprised. "Not a very flattering photograph, but it is mine," he said.

She held the wallet in her hand, reading his name, then raised her eyes to his face. He could have sworn that there was a flicker of admiration in them before she flipped his wallet closed.

"So it is. Well, Mr. Garrett." She handed the wallet back to him. "Unless you know a very good forger, you seem to be with the *Times,* just as you said."

"I never lie." He had the good grace to stick his tongue in his cheek as he said it. Then, linking his arm through hers, he began to lead her off to the terrace. In the background, a Johnny Mathis song was just beginning. "Now, about that pain..."

She laughed, her body leaning into his. "I recommend dancing to ease it."

He couldn't think of a better way to hold her in his arms. "Dancing?"

Sheila nodded. She could feel her blood begin to rush, a prophecy of things to come. "Uh-huh. And preferably in the moonlight."

He looked up. Above them the sky was black as velvet with a smattering of tiny silvery pinholes punched into it in various places. "Well, I'll be. Just what the doctor ordered."

Slade slipped his fingers through Sheila's, linking them together as he drew her closer to him. They began to sway ever so slightly to the music that had followed them out.

"Yes," Sheila murmured, her voice low and silky, "it is."

He breathed in the heady scent from her hair as she rested her head against his shoulder and wondered how he'd managed to slip into heaven without knowing that he had died.

It was an evening that began with a smile and ended with far more than that in a tiny cove on a private beach not too far away from the hospital that the fund-raiser was attempting to benefit that night. Sheila knew the owners, who were conveniently away on a trip.

He hadn't known that it was possible to feel this way about a woman, to find so many layers of enjoyment in such a small space of time.

Shrouded by the moonlight, in his arms, Sheila had been everything he had ever wanted in a woman. Given him everything he could have ever hoped for. More.

And less.

Less, because she had asked for nothing in return while silently giving everything to him that a woman could. Her body, her soul. He couldn't ever remember responding like this, being both master and slave, lover and the one loved. It was like falling under a spell. Like magic. He was convinced that there was no other word for it, save for that.

Magic.

What had happened to him, between them, fueled his dreams for months afterward. More than once, the memory he kept pressed close to his heart had given him the only solace in a world gone mad.

They'd talked and made love all night. He'd left Sheila in the parking lot of the hotel at dawn the next day, knowing that for a brief moment in time, they had been each other's soul mates. Knowing, too, without it ever having been said, that for both of them that small island of time they had shared had been different.

So here he was, about to "look her up" after all this time. What if she wasn't as wonderful as he'd remembered?

What if she was?

And after he saw her, then what? Would he suggest having dinner? After having made love with her beneath a blanket of stars, dinner somehow seemed far too mundane and ordinary a way to go.

And yet, Slade instinctively knew that with Sheila nothing could be mundane and ordinary.

He tugged on his pocket and then cursed roundly when his fingers came in contact with only material. Damn, but he was making noises like some love-struck puppy rather than a hardened, thirty-three-year-old journalist who had kicked around the world a number of times.

Johnny Mathis's voice had faded away on a lyrical note. A fast-talking deejay was hawking a contest and laughing at his own nonstop patter. Slade snapped off the radio and rubbed a hand over his chin again. This wasn't like him, hesitating like this.

Just what was he afraid of? It wasn't as if he was about to meet his destiny. That only waited on the battlefields.

No time like the present to see if his dream would dissolve on contact like cheap dish detergent at the first sign of crockery.

Unfolding his long, lanky frame, he got out of his sports car and slammed the door closed. The lock snapped on automatically.

Anticipation heightened his heart rate. He felt the way he had six months ago while waiting to meet a source on the back streets of what was left of downtown Beirut.

Stepping aside for an elderly couple, Slade walked into the medical building's sun-filled lobby. There was a pharmacy on the right, its window lined with a gay array of stuffed animals guaranteed to take a small child's mind off the pending visit to the doctor. It was doing a fair amount of business. On the left, next to the elevators, were two large black boards encased in glass.

Slade scanned the names on the directory until he found hers: Pollack, Dr. Sheila. Suite 812.

Probably had a good view of Catalina from her window, he mused, pressing for the elevator.

He thought it both annoying and amusing that his palm was damp.

By the time the elevator arrived, he wasn't alone. Three other people had joined him, and just as the doors began to close, a woman ran up, dragging a child in her wake. The doors shuddered open again, and then closed in earnest. The little boy fidgeted and wiggled against Slade's leg. The boy's mother looked harried. It made him glad he didn't have any kids of his own.

Slade watched the digital numbers change shape overhead, holding his breath without realizing it.

He'd woken up at two in the morning to the sound of bombs bursting overhead, had run from sniper fire through a city street reduced to rubble, and had lived with refugees in the mountains, sharing their meager food and even more meager dreams for peace, just to get a story. Running on adrenaline and little else, Slade couldn't remember feeling uneasy during any of those times.

Then why should he feel that way now, simply riding up in an elevator?

He supposed the answer was because none of that had seemed very real to him at the time. It was almost as if he were reading about his life right along with the rest of the *Times*'s readership.

This, however, had an Andy-Hardy-talks-to-the-judge quality to it that brought it all vividly home to him.

You could take the boy out of the small town, Slade thought, passingly amused, but you couldn't take the small town out of the boy.

He was the last one off the elevator on eight. There were no other floors. There was no more wasting time. Just as the doors shut behind him, Slade debated riding down again and forgetting the whole thing. After all, he reasoned, a dream could continue as long as it wasn't disproven. As long as nothing came along to make it burst apart.

Coward's way, he upbraided himself silently. And it had been a long time since he had permitted himself to be a coward. There was no room for it in his life.

Arrows on the wall above a sign told him which direction to take. He made a left at the end of a long, slender corridor.

Her office was in the middle of the hall. Suite 812. Dr. Sheila Pollack, Ob-Gyn, the plaque proclaimed. He was vaguely aware of soft music coming from inside the room.

Slade wondered if she'd be surprised to see him standing here. God knew, he was surprised to see himself standing here.

Feeling like he was invading a foreign country, he turned the doorknob and walked in.

The reception area was spacious, with light blue walls adding a sense of tranquillity. There were ten straight-back, light blue upholstered chairs with highly polished, stained ash arms that were shaped like curled talons, five on either side of a marble-topped coffee table. The effect was more reminiscent of an old world salon where people gathered to exchange ideas than a doctor's office.

It reminded him of her.

He approached the desk and knocked on the closed frosted glass window. The nurse who opened it looked at him curiously. She glanced down to see if he was holding anything in his hand.

Probably thought he was a pharmaceutical salesman, Slade guessed. "Hi, is Dr. Pollack in?"

"Yes," replied the nurse, Lisa according to the name pinned on her crisp white uniform. She waited patiently for him to continue.

A little of his own impatience surfaced. "Well, could I see her?"

Lisa wondered if he had read the sign on the door. "Um, maybe you're looking for Dr. Theodore Pollack," she suggested politely. "Sixth floor. Room number—"

Theodore Pollack? The name was vaguely familiar, but he couldn't remember where he'd heard it before. Slade wondered if Theodore was her husband and if he'd been entertaining a married woman in his dreams. And for one magnificent night, in his arms.

"No, it's Sheila Pollack I want to see." He glanced behind him. There were three women in the office, all very pregnant. His mouth curved slightly. "Off the record."

That was an odd way to put it, Lisa thought, then understood. "Oh, you mean personally."

"Yes."

Very personally, he thought, feeling a longing traveling through him. God, the next thing that was going to happen was that he'd start breaking out like some pubescent teenager.

Lisa looked at him uncertainly. The doctor would have mentioned someone like this if she was expecting him, wouldn't she? She glanced over her shoulder involuntarily. "She's busy now."

Well, he'd waited this long, he could wait a little while longer. He supposed he couldn't expect to go in just like that.

Slade nodded, resigning himself to the fact. "I'll wait."

He looked completely out of place in the waiting room, Lisa thought. She rose from her chair. "Can I tell her who's waiting?"

"Sure." He picked up a business magazine just to give his hands something to do. "Tell her it's someone who would like another dance in the moonlight when she's free."

One of the women behind him laughed softly. He smiled in response as he turned to sit down. He looked at the woman fleetingly, and she blushed in response.

Lisa slid the frosted glass closed again. She excused herself after the fact and disappeared into one of the inner rooms.

Chapter Two

Sheila carefully placed the tissue sample she'd just taken from her patient onto the sterile glass slide and sealed it. Only then did she glance up to see why one of her nurses had entered the room during an examination after only a perfunctory knock, without waiting to be told to come in.

Lisa looked confused, Sheila thought. The young nurse had been with her since she had set up her practice across the street from Harris Memorial. Very little tended to rattle her. That something had now piqued Sheila's curiosity.

Pushing away from the metal stirrups, Sheila rose gingerly from her stool. "What's the matter, Lisa? Is someone throwing up on one of the chairs again?"

The last time had been so bad, the cleaning service hadn't been able to save it. She'd had to have the chair reupholstered. Given the heavy traffic of pregnant women she had been seeing lately, she was surprised it didn't happen more frequently. Plastic slipcovers might have been an alternative if she didn't hate the idea so much. Half her patients were uncomfortable enough without having to unstick themselves from the furniture whenever they got up.

Lisa shook her head in response, then waited a moment before she answered. She glanced uncertainly at the doctor's patient and lowered her voice. "There's a man in the waiting room. He wants to see you."

That wasn't so unusual, Sheila mused. She placed the slide on the counter beside its label. The pickup from the lab was at three. She had to remember to give the slide to Ruth to add to the collection.

"With his wife?" she asked absently.

"No."

Sheila shrugged as she put the slide into the bubble-lined manila envelope. "Maybe he wants to see my father."

It wouldn't be the first time a new patient would wander into the wrong office by mistake. When her mother had had her office in the same building, mix-ups occurred with a fair amount of regularity.

Lisa shook her head. "I already gave him that choice. He wants to see you."

On occasion Sheila found herself in the position of having to assuage a nervous husband's fears. Not everyone greeted pregnancy with optimism and open arms. Sometimes husbands turned out to be more frightened than their wives about what lay ahead in the coming months before delivery. Sheila supposed she could give the man a few minutes between patients, provided his questions were simple and few. Otherwise, she'd have to see him after hours.

Provided she had after hours, she thought, unconsciously rubbing her stomach. She'd already had false labor pains once, and had checked herself into the hospital last week just in case. Today the pains felt worse, more intense, as if they were all building up toward a huge finale.

Sheila washed her hands, then dried them. A pink paper towel fluttered into the wastebasket. "Did he give you a name?"

"No. He said to tell you that he'd like another dance in the moonlight when you have the time." Lisa held her breath as she watched Sheila's face for a reaction.

Heart thudding madly against her ribs, Sheila almost knocked the baby monitor off the counter. Flashing her patient a quick smile, she barely whispered, "I'll just be a minute," before taking Lisa out into the hall.

It couldn't be.

And yet, it had to be. Coincidence only stretched so far. Besides, who else would have asked about a dance in the moonlight?

Sheila immediately looked toward the reception area, but the sliding frosted glass windowpane was closed, blocking her view of the waiting room. All she saw were misty shapes that could have been anyone.

But one of them belonged to him. She'd swear to it.

Slade.

She wasn't prepared to entertain specters from her past right now. She had patients and pain to deal with. She took hold of Lisa's arm.

"This man, what does he look like?" Lisa winced and Sheila realized that she was holding on too tightly. Chagrined, she dropped her hand.

Lisa wasn't aware that she sighed before answering, but Sheila was. It gave Sheila her answer before Lisa even opened her mouth. "Kind of craggy, but good-looking. Very good-looking."

That would be the way to describe him, Sheila thought. Craggy but good-looking. Bone-meltingly good-looking. "About six-two, brown eyes, dark brown hair, lopsided smile?" She didn't know why she was bothering to ask. It *had* to be him.

Lisa did her best to remember the order of the questions. "Yes, yes, yes, and he didn't smile." Not that she hadn't wanted him to, Lisa thought.

"Lucky you," Sheila murmured more to herself than to the nurse.

It was his smile more than anything else that had caused her to throw common sense and caution to the winds and do what she'd done, becoming Cathy to his Heathcliff, Katharine Hepburn to his Spencer Tracy.

She should have had her head examined.

And yet, she wouldn't have changed a damn thing even if she could. She was always going to remember that night, and cherish the child who had been created even though it had been completely by accident, despite precautions taken.

Lisa studied her face, wondering if Sheila was going into labor. "Doctor, are you all right? You look a little pale."

"I always look pale when I'm entertaining the Ghost of Christmas Past," she answered, distracted.

She never thought she was going to see him again, and now he was here, in her waiting room. What was she going to do?

Sheila stopped. There was no reason to feel this panicky sensation scrambling through her like a spider sliding off a slick mirror. She had made a mature decision after her world had suddenly been upended and she found herself pregnant.

Up until the moment she read the result of the pregnancy test, she had never dreamed of having a child of her own. Her own childhood had convinced her that a successful career did not leave any room for having a family. At least, not one that would receive the kind of attention she always believed a family merited.

But finding herself on the other side of the examining table had evoked such maternal feelings within her that she couldn't just ignore them or erase them. Suddenly sprouting full grown within her breast, they clamored for release. She wanted this baby.

She was having this baby, she had thought fiercely. And she was having it alone, without benefit of spouse or "significant other."

The significant other in this case was a man she considered to be her star-crossed lover. The evening had been far too perfect to ruin with a second encounter, much less adding the news of a "dividend" resulting from the night of lovemaking to that encounter. She knew that would have put everything into a different perspective, dulling the sparkle by introducing reality.

During that night, Sheila felt that she had gotten to know Slade as well as any woman could know a man. He was as fiercely independent as she was, and as content with his lifestyle as she was with hers. Neither of them wanted commitment, much less children, in the picture.

Knowing this had convinced Sheila not to attempt to locate Slade to let him know that he was going to be a father.

There would have been no point to it. She didn't need him to make the picture complete. She had herself to rely on. And in times of need, there were also her parents to turn to. They had taken the news surprisingly well, acting every bit as sophisticated about it as they did about everything else.

Theodore and Susan Pollack might not have given her a fairy-tale childhood, or even a traditional one, but they were making up for it by being there for her now. Because of them and her own outlook, Sheila had quickly adjusted to the situation. The road was a little bumpy at times, but she always handled it.

And now he was out there, in her waiting room. Waiting.

And here she was, almost nine months' pregnant with his baby. Talk about throwing a monkey wrench into the works.

Sheila pressed her lips together. She had a patient still waiting on the table in the room behind her, shivering under a yellow-and-white-checkered sheet. Not to mention two more patients she hadn't even seen yet in examining rooms two and three, plus a full schedule for the remainder of the afternoon. This was no time for personal complications.

She curved her hand around her protruding belly. She had enough of those to deal with as it was. All she wanted to do right now was see her patients and wait out these new twinges she was experiencing.

Lisa touched her arm. "Maybe I should tell him to come back later?"

Yes, like the Twelfth of Never. Right along with Johnny Mathis.

"No, just tell him that if this isn't about one of my patients going into labor, he's going to have to wait until I'm finished seeing the rest of my patients."

And maybe by then, he'd go away on his own. And then they could both go on living with their keepsake fantasies of that magical night.

Lisa nodded uncertainly and slipped out of the room. "All right, I'll tell him."

Mallory Flannigan turned around at the sound of the door opening again. The paper cover rustled beneath her. "Problem?"

"Nothing I can't handle," Sheila answered cheerfully. *Or so I'd like to think.*

Mallory wasn't altogether convinced. There was something in her doctor's voice that made her think something was rattling her normally unflappable physician. Their association went beyond that of doctor and patient. Among other things, Mallory, a real estate agent, had sold Sheila the house she was living in. And Sheila had provided her with a shoulder to lean on when Mallory had gone through her own difficult time. She would have liked to return the favor.

Pulling the thin cloth back, she waited as Sheila's long, cool fingers lightly skimmed her breasts and checked her over.

Sheila nodded to herself, satisfied with the result. There appeared to be nothing to worry about. "You're fine, Mallory. The tenderness you're experiencing is common." She took Mallory's chart out and wrote a few notes down on a fresh piece of paper. "It should pass soon."

Mallory sat up. She'd thought as much, but it never hurt to check. She pulled the robe up around her. Yellow-and-white checkers were definitely not her style, she mused. Biting her lip, she debated intruding. The debate lasted less than a second. She liked Sheila too much to stand on formality.

"You know, when I was so upset about Jackson leaving and then coming back into my life, you practically had a stranglehold on me to get me to talk."

Sheila made another note, then put down the pen. She smiled. That had turned out well. She doubted her own situation would follow suit. In this case, she had no idea what "well" constituted.

"Yes, and as I remember, you didn't. You wanted to work things out on your own."

Sheila's manner, light and friendly, still warned Mallory not to interfere. Mallory rarely paid attention to warnings, especially not where friends were concerned. "That was what I was going to tell you. Things do work out on their own if you just give them their head."

Sheila picked up the chart and rested it against her belly. She was going to miss her little shelf once this was over.

"I'll remember that." *In this case, it doesn't apply, but I'll remember, anyway.*

Mallory was far from convinced, but for now, she let the subject drop. She knew by her own example that you couldn't coerce these things from people, it had to come voluntarily.

She slid off the table, her toes curled as they touched the cold floor. "Well, if you need to talk, or want a sounding board, I'll be more than happy to volunteer. And even if you don't, I'd still like to invite you to my wedding."

Sheila paused by the door, surprised. And pleased. "Wedding?"

"Yes, Jackson and I are getting married in three weeks or so." She knew her voice was filled with pride, and she didn't care how chauvinistic that sounded. "Joshua is going to be best man."

"Won't be the first time the best man wasn't able to stand up at the wedding." Sheila laughed. She had helped bring Mallory's son Joshua into the world only last month. In her experience it had been one of the fastest deliveries she had ever had the pleasure to be present at.

"In this case, Marlene's housekeeper will be holding him," Mallory said, mentioning another one of Sheila's patients, a woman she had gotten close to during their enforced stay in the waiting room. "I'll send you an invitation to make it official," she promised. "As soon as I have a fixed date myself."

"I'll be looking for it," Sheila assured her.

She closed the door behind her as she entered the hall. A wedding, she thought, allowing herself a touch of envy. Well, a wedding wasn't in her future, but she was really happy for Mallory. She'd seen Jackson at the delivery, and he looked as if he was capable of making Mallory very happy.

It was nice to know that some people were experiencing happy endings.

Sheila glanced at Lisa. The nurse was bent over the appointment book, doing some juggling. She had already informed Lisa that she was going to have to switch some of her patients over to her partner, Dr. Kelly, for the time being. Having resisted it all along, she was finally slowing down.

The frosted glass window was still closed. Sheila knew Lisa did it in order to concentrate on her work, but she wished it was open just this once.

No, she didn't.

Squaring her shoulders, Sheila went on to her next examining room. A small, sharp pain rippled down her spine. She ignored it. If she had begun to wonder about every little pain she had, she would have remained flat on her back the entire nine months. Work was far more therapeutic.

Three hours later, Sheila found herself out of patients. The waiting room, save for Slade, Lisa had informed her, was empty.

"Are you sure?" Sheila asked.

Lisa nodded. "No one. Just him and a lot of magazines with tired pages."

"No calls from the hospital?" A hopeful note entered her voice.

"No calls," Lisa confirmed. What was there between the doctor and the man out in the waiting room? Lisa exchanged looks with one of the other nurses as the thought hit her. This was the baby's father. It had to be. She'd never seen Dr. Pollack so uneasy.

Feeling suddenly protective, Lisa placed her hand over Sheila's. "I can tell him that you were called away."

She was tempted, but then Sheila shook her head. It would only be postponing the inevitable. He had to find out sometime, she supposed. But she had been thinking more along the lines of during the baby's college graduation, just before he or she delivered the valedictorian speech.

"No, show him into the office." Sighing, she turned toward the room at the rear of the short hall. "I might as well get this over with."

Feeling more tired than she had in a long time, Sheila walked into her office and sat down behind her desk. She wished that it was higher, or her seat was lower. Or, for the first time since she had conducted her own pregnancy test in this very office, that the result had been something different than it was.

She really wasn't looking forward to having to tell Slade Garrett that she was carrying his child.

The man she had made love with had taken on almost superhuman qualities, qualities only enhanced by the passage of time. It wasn't anything he could live up to in person. She didn't expect him to, but neither did she want to give up the magical essence of that night. Having it exposed to the reality of day-to-day life would take away the unique qualities it now possessed.

She sighed again, waiting for Slade to enter.

He had run out of things to read half an hour ago and given up editing the articles in his head long before then. During the last three hours, he had endured the curious glances of a parade of patients who had disappeared behind a door he wasn't allowed to open. Now the room was finally empty. At a quarter past five, he didn't expect anyone else to come in for an appointment.

Slade heard the inner door opening and rose, towering over the nurse who entered. The one who had taken his message in to Sheila. He glanced at her name tag.

"My turn, Lisa?" he asked gamely.

There was something about the man's brown eyes that made Lisa have to remind herself to breathe. After a beat, she nodded. "Yes. The doctor will see you now."

"Very sporting of her," Slade said cryptically.

He had no idea why he hadn't walked out an hour ago. His job called for patience, but he had never grown accustomed to exercising it. Waiting made him irritable. But curiosity had bound him to the chair.

He'd had three hours to dwell on the image in his mind and wonder if she could live up to it. He doubted it, but he had to see for himself. He figured he owed it to both of them.

There had been one instance, months ago, when a sniper had killed his guide and narrowly missed killing him, during which his life had passed before his eyes. He'd seen

Sheila then, just the way she'd been on the beach, bathed in moonlight and his gaze, nothing more. The image had burned itself into his mind even after he'd reached sanctuary.

No other woman had ever had such a profound, lasting impression on him. He had to find out if it had been just the intensity of the situation, or if there was more between them than an incredibly passionate night.

He followed the nurse to the last room in the back. "Ah, the inner sanctum."

The nurse murmured something as she stepped back, but he didn't catch it. He wondered about the strange look in her eyes and the way the other two nurses had looked at him as he passed by. He couldn't be the first man to walk in here, Slade thought.

He ran his hand along the back of his neck. It felt itchy, the way it always did just before he walked into an unexpected situation. Turning the doorknob, he entered her office.

She was there, sitting behind her desk. The darkening blue sky seemed to intensify her blondness and the white of her smock. Her hands were folded primly before her as if she was a student in some private school classroom, waiting for the teacher to enter.

Fantasies began taking hold again. She was just as beautiful as he remembered.

More.

Damn her.

"I like your waiting room." He nodded behind him, his eyes on hers. Something was different about her. There was something in her eyes, he realized. Fear? Defiance? He couldn't quite identify it. "You don't believe in furniture that swallows you up."

She smiled as nerves clenched and unclenched in her stomach. He was more tanned than he'd been before, and his hair was a little longer than it had been that night. But her memory hadn't lied. If anything, it had faded. He was even better-looking than she remembered. She hadn't thought that was possible.

She pressed her hands closer together. "It makes it difficult for the pregnant women if they have to dig themselves out of chairs that absorb them like huge melted marshmallows." Her tone matched his. Glib, yet with a thread of tension. "So, how have you been?"

Before he had a chance to answer, very deliberately, she unfolded her hands and leaned back in the chair.

She saw his jaw slacken as his eyes rested on the swell of her belly.

Whatever answer he had for her was lost as he stared at her. God, this was one cool lady. He masked his reaction as best he could. "Fine, when I wasn't being shot at."

No surprise. Nothing. She felt a little disappointed, she realized. "Remind me to play poker with you the next time you get up a game."

He laughed shortly. "Sorry, you just took me by surprise. I tend to numb out then."

Something tightened, hot and painful, in his gut. Automatically, Slade glanced at her hand. There was no ring on it, but maybe the rock her husband had given her was too large for her to wear during working hours. It would undoubtedly get stuck in the rubber gloves she had to pull on.

"I guess congratulations are in order." That made the joke on him, he thought. He'd been having fantasies about a married, pregnant woman.

His voice sounded strange, hollow. "You mean because of the baby?"

It seemed to be a part-and-parcel deal. "I mean the wedding."

She stared at him, uncomprehending. "What wedding?"

Why was she playing it so coy? She looked large enough to burst. Maybe he was being unreasonable, but he felt a little cheated. "Yours."

Sheila blinked, confused. What was he talking about? She raised her brow, a smile playing on her lips. "Am I getting married?"

This was the nineties, he reminded himself. Old-fashioned, traditional views existed right beside comfortable, newly forged ones. But he would have thought, since she was a doctor with a position on the staff of one of the most respected hospitals in the country, that she would have gotten married, either before or after the fact.

He drew closer. "Then you're not—?"

"Married?" He nodded. Sheila rose, feeling just the slightest bit hemmed in. "No."

It didn't make sense to him. She hadn't struck him as the type to thumb her nose at society. "Then how—?"

He *was* putting her on, wasn't he? "I would think a man in your position and with your expertise would know how."

Slade studied her face. He reached for his pocket before he silently cursed himself and tobacco leaves in general for ever having existed.

Suddenly, his brain swiftly began sliding down an entirely different path. "How far along are you?" he asked quietly.

So, it was beginning to dawn on him, was it? She didn't know if he was being incredibly slow, or just in denial.

"About as far as I can go," she answered briskly. She wanted out of this conversation and wished the telephone would ring. Where were emergency deliveries when you needed them? "Nine months."

Nine months. Wow. He perched on the side of the desk, because right now he wasn't completely certain if his legs could support him. "Then that would make the baby—"

"Yours," she completed for him. That wasn't panic in his eyes, but what was it? "Yes."

"Wow." He ran his hand over his neck. The itching had stopped. "What a welcome-home present."

She couldn't help laughing. He looked utterly stunned. "You're turning pale."

A baby. She was having a baby. *He* was having a baby. Sort of. Slade blew out a breath and fervently wished for a cigarette. Just one. "Just a little overwhelmed, that's all."

Yes, she would have expected that. "You don't have to be."

He waved her into silence. He'd deal with what he did have to be and didn't have to be later. There was a more important question crowding his mind. "Why didn't you tell me?"

She shrugged, not certain she liked his tone. She definitely didn't like the way she was feeling right now. A little liquidy and out of it. It was hard to concentrate. "There was no way to reach you, and besides, we're both adults—"

His eyes dipped down to the swell of her abdomen. "Obviously."

No, she didn't like his tone, she decided. She didn't know why she was attempting to relieve him of his responsibility in this. Maybe because she didn't like depending on anyone for anything. "I'm perfectly capable of taking care of a baby on my own."

He hadn't thought she was the type to climb up on a soapbox. He laced his fingers together and continued watching her as she moved around the office. "But it is mine."

She supposed she could see why he would doubt it. The hurt that she felt was totally uncalled-for. But it was there, anyway. "Yes."

He watched her eyes as she answered. "You're sure?"

The hurt mushroomed into anger. She struggled to control it. When she spoke, it was in a measured cadence that only hinted at the fire beneath.

"We had a very unique situation. You did sweep me off my feet, so to speak." Literally at one point, as well as otherwise. "But don't get any ideas. I don't sleep around." The fierceness left her voice as she placed a supporting hand against her back. It was really beginning to ache. "These days, I don't even sleep." Her throat felt dry. She thought longingly of the bottled water in the snack area's refrigerator.

He was still a little stunned. "But I used—"

Yes, even in the heat of the moment, they had practiced safe sex. That was the irony of it. She shrugged. "These things happen. It is your baby."

He believed her. Not because he very much wanted to, but because he saw the truth in her eyes. "All right. Then marry me."

Stunned, she was only glad that she hadn't been drinking water. She would have choked on it. "Excuse me?"

"If this is my baby—" Slade saw her brow rise and regrouped "—since this is my baby, I have a responsibility toward it. I think we should get married."

They weren't the words she expected to hear from a free spirit like Slade. Now that she had, they annoyed her. Where did he get off, deciding all three of their futures just like that, without even consulting her?

"The reason I didn't even try to get in contact with you, Slade, is because I don't need your proposal or your 'responsibility.' I can take care of this baby very well on my own. Financially and emotionally."

"But it is mine." He pointed out the obvious. "You just admitted it. That means I have some say in the situation."

She crossed her arms before her. "And what is it that you'd like to say?"

He'd just said it, he thought. He'd asked her to marry him. Maybe she needed it clarified. "I think a baby deserves to have a family."

Mommy and Daddy and baby did not make instant family in her book. She knew better. "When he is old enough, he can have one."

"He?" Was she telling him that it was a boy?

"Or she," Sheila amended, reading his thoughts. "No, I haven't had an amniocentesis. Some things, I like being surprised with."

Talk about surprise. Slade felt as if he had been hit over the head with a two-by-four. But he wanted to do the right thing. "We have to talk."

She felt the twinges growing harder and knew exactly what was going on. She was getting her emergency delivery, all right. She had to get him out of here.

"Right now, what we have to do is say goodbye. I have rounds to make, so if you'll excuse me." Firmly taking his arm, she all but pushed him out into the hall.

"But—"

She closed the door in Slade's face. With a deep sigh, she leaned against it. Chewing on her lip, Sheila counted mentally.

Yup, no mistake about it. She was in labor. For real, this time.

Chapter Three

The contractions were coming hard and strong. There was no comparison between what she'd felt a week ago and what was happening now. This was definitely the real thing.

Not long now, she thought.

"Looks like you're going to be an early bird," Sheila murmured to the infant in her stomach, "like your mom."

She looked toward the door, tempted for a moment to go after Slade. She forced herself to lock the feeling away. Her first decision had been the right one. She was doing this on her own.

"I have no idea what your dad is like, except for sexy and pushy. Very sexy," she whispered just before another good-size wave of pain made its presence known.

It left her breathless. She had to wait a moment before she could make her way over to her desk and the telephone. Perspiration, in defiance to the cool temperature in the room, was beginning to bead around her hairline.

At least the baby had obligingly waited until she was finished with the day's appointments, Sheila mused as she tapped out the direct number to Harris Memorial's Admitting desk.

Someone picked up after the second ring. "Admitting. This is Rosa Martinez. How may I help you?"

Sheila grimaced as she felt the ghost of another contraction approaching.

You can have this baby for me.

She let out a shaky breath. "This is Dr. Sheila Pollack. I think it's time I made use of that room I've been reserving."

She heard the staccato tapping of a computer keyboard before the woman responded. Obviously Rosa was pulling her name up from the data bank.

"Now, Doctor?"

"Oh, yes, most definitely now." Sheila held her hand over her belly, as if that could somehow ease the pain. So this was what labor really felt like. She couldn't say she much cared for it.

"Terrific. I win the pool," she heard the woman on the other end exclaim gleefully. Sheila was vaguely aware that a pool had been in existence concerning her due date ever since she'd had the false labor pains last week. "Um, sorry, Doctor. I just got a little excited. I've never won anything before."

Sheila managed a laugh. She thought about sitting down, but rejected the idea. If she sat down, she might not be able to get up again without help.

"That's all right. Nice to know I've brightened someone's day, although I wouldn't collect just yet if I were you." The pains made her feel as if she was going to give birth any minute, but she knew better than to assume it would be that simple. "The baby might be slow and decide to hang in until tomorrow."

The woman responded to Sheila's friendly manner, becoming chatty. "Not a chance, Doctor. Not if it's your baby. Everyone says that you do everything fast. That's why the nurses all like you. You don't drag things out. My sister works on the maternity floor, and she says—''

Sheila pressed her lips together, sealing in a surprised cry. She hardly heard anything the woman was saying. Light-headed, she forced herself to concentrate on the voice.

''Rosa?''

The woman stopped rambling. ''Yes, Doctor?''

''I should be there in a few minutes.'' She had to catch Lisa or one of the others before they left. The hospital was only down the block and across the street, but right now, she was incapable of walking the distance, and she wasn't too sure if she could even drive it. ''Maybe longer.''

She squeezed out the final words as she dropped the telephone receiver. It slid into the wastepaper basket. Sheila gripped the top of her desk, bracing herself.

This one was the papa bear of contractions, she thought as it closed its steely jaws on her.

The world around her was enshrouded by a milky curtain. Or was she the one encased in it? All she knew was that she felt like fainting.

Perspiration slid in a zigzag pattern down her spine, leaving a damp trail in its wake to mark its path. *Please, don't let me pass out.*

With effort, she reeled in the receiver and replaced it on the cradle. Sheila didn't notice the door opening behind her until Slade was in the room beside her.

Debating with himself, Slade had made it all the way to the elevator before he'd turned around on his heel and returned. He was going with his instincts, with what he felt was right. His instincts had never failed him before.

''Look, I'm not taking no for an answer,'' Slade said to her back. ''I want to give this baby a name.''

Oh, great, him again. Just what I need right now, an argument.

''The baby will have one,'' she ground out between clenched teeth. ''Mine.''

He placed his hands on her shoulders, wanting to turn her around to face him. The material felt damp to the touch. He was vaguely conscious of thinking that it wasn't hot in here. Why was she perspiring?

"I want to marry you, Sheila. I want to marry you before the baby's born."

She let him turn her around because she didn't have the strength to resist. "Too late."

Her complexion was ghostly pale, and she was perspiring. He found himself holding on to her because he was afraid she'd fall if he let go. "Are you in labor?"

"Nice deduction, Sherlock," she whispered. "I can see why the paper is so impressed with your razor-sharp mind."

She almost whimpered as another pain slammed into her, skimming across her loins with finely sharpened ice skates, but she managed to muffle the sound at the last moment.

"Yes, I'm in labor."

The next sensation she experienced had Sheila glancing down at the carpet. There was a small, almost imperceptible, damp spot directly by her foot. Her water had broken.

Sheila sighed. "It's official."

He'd been in far more dire situations than this, although he'd never helped a woman give birth before. The thought made him a little uneasy. Slade forced his voice to sound calm.

"All the more reason to make an honest woman out of you."

She rolled her eyes and only partially from the pain. Sheila tried unsuccessfully to gain the door. Her legs weren't cooperating.

Frustration elbowed its way into her tone. "You didn't tell me you had a corny side to you, Garrett." The next moment, she grasped his hand, squeezing his fingers hard as she tried to steady herself.

"You never asked."

Unclenching her hand, Sheila breathed a sigh of relief. It had passed. With luck, the next few wouldn't be as intense. All she needed was just a little time to get to the hospital, nothing more. Just a little time. That wasn't so much to ask, was it?

Her body told her that it might be.

Taking charge, Slade slipped a supporting arm around her waist. "Okay, let's go."

She didn't like being commandeered. Besides, Slade wasn't the traveling companion she'd had in mind. "Go where?"

Was she kidding, or trying to prove something? "To the hospital. You're having a baby."

A slight smile curved her mouth automatically. "Thank you for pointing that out. It might have escaped me, otherwise."

He looked around for her purse. He didn't see one and abandoned the thought. They probably all knew who she was at the hospital, anyway. Her nurses could take care of the small details.

Slade edged her over toward the door, shortening his stride to match the small steps she was taking. "You always this testy?"

Yes, she supposed she must have sounded that way. "Only when I'm about to give birth." Her eyes apologized to him, even if she couldn't say the words. "Look, you don't have to do this. One of the nurses'll drive me over. It's only a block away." Sheila winced before she could finish. Only pride prevented her from doubling over.

The woman had a stubborn streak a mile wide. At any other time, he might have found it challenging or even amusing. But not right now.

"Humor me, Sheila. I always wanted to have a reason to speed in Newport."

"For a block? Wonderful. I'm having a baby and you want to try out for the Indy 500." She wanted to stride out of the office, the way she always did, but she couldn't. She could hardly walk, although she didn't want to admit it.

Slade shrugged good-naturedly as they entered the hall. "Everyone's got to have a fantasy."

The other nurses had left for the night. Concerned about Sheila, Lisa had remained. She wanted to see Sheila leave the office before she went home herself.

She jumped to her feet when she saw Sheila emerging. One look at Sheila's face and she was hurrying over to her side. *Oh, God, this is it,* she thought.

"Are you all right, Doctor?"

I've been better. Sheila glanced at Slade. *A lot better.*

"Actually," she said as a huge sigh escaped her lips, "I'm going to have a baby."

Slade ushered her to the outer door. He glanced at Lisa over his shoulder. "After we get married."

"Doctor?" Lisa looked after her uncertainly.

"Don't worry, I can take care of myself." She was referring to Slade, not her condition, when she said it. "I've already called Admitting. Do me a favor, tell Dr. Kelly he's on for tonight."

Lisa nodded, running back to her desk.

"Efficient, even in pain," Slade commented. "Admirable."

"Necessary," she corrected him. The elevator was only a few steps from her office. Why did it seem so far away? Sheila looked at him suspiciously as they reached the metal doors. "You're not planning on driving me to a church, are you?"

Slade pressed for the elevator. He no sooner removed his finger from the button than the car arrived, its doors yawning open. He kept one hand on the gunmetal gray door as he ushered Sheila inside.

"No, but the hospital has a chapel." He saw suspicion flower into alarm in her eyes. Slade continued mildly, "I know, last year I interviewed the priest who officiates there.

He's usually around somewhere in the building in the afternoons."

She wished that there were still metal railings around the inside perimeter of the car. But the elevators had all been renovated. She had nothing to hold on to but Slade, and she wasn't comfortable about that right now.

"Good for him," she muttered.

The elevator went straight down to the first floor, for once without stopping to pick up any passengers.

"Can you walk?" Slade asked when the doors opened again. His car was a long way off, and he didn't want to leave Sheila just standing here alone while he went to get it.

The pain had temporarily left, allowing her a respite. A little of her strength returned.

"Right now, I'm thinking of running." She grew serious. The only thing she knew about Slade was what he had told her. What if it was all a lie? It wouldn't have been the first time she had been lied to, she thought, remembering her residency. What if she had made love with a crazy man? One of those obsessive-compulsives types? "You can't force me to marry you."

He looked at Sheila as he led her toward his car. She couldn't read what was in his eyes. "I wouldn't think I'd have to. I would have thought that your common sense would have prevailed."

For a journalist, he'd certainly chosen the wrong phrase to support his point. She laughed softly to herself. At herself. And him.

"If I'd had common sense, Garrett, I wouldn't have gone dancing on the beach in the moonlight—" Even as she said it, she couldn't force herself to regret that night, or anything that had resulted because of it. Her mouth curved as she continued, "Wound up getting sand in my clothes, among other things."

Just to hear her talk about it, even in passing, brought that night vividly back to him. His smile was soft, reminiscent. "It's called making memories."

Yes, it was, but saying so would only give him ammunition for his side. And there was no way she was going to marry him. Not because some infinitesimal part of her didn't long for it, but because it just wouldn't be right. Not for her.

The pain was starting again. She could hardly feel her feet making contact with the ground as she walked. Where the hell had he parked? Portland?

"Whatever it's called, I don't want to compound a mistake by making another one."

He noticed she was gritting her teeth again, and he tried to move her along as quickly as possible.

"Is that what you think this is?" His eyes swept over her abdomen. "A mistake?"

No, never that. But she wanted to make him understand. "Intellectually, I wasn't in the right time or place to begin a family. I'm still not," she added in a moment of weakness.

Slade stopped by his car, quickly unlocking the passenger door.

"Well, something obviously was." He held Sheila's hands as she lowered herself into the seat. A sports car wasn't the most comfortable mode of transportation for her. "And I'm not talking about intellectually, I'm talking about emotionally." He pulled the seat belt out as far as it could go and offered the metal clip to her. "How do you feel emotionally?"

"Like I'm about to scream." She grasped his hand as well as the clip and squeezed hard. She held on to him until the wave passed. "Boy, those pains are sharp."

Gingerly, he uncoupled himself from her. "So are your nails." He could see the imprint of all five tips on his skin.

Sheila waited until he'd taken his seat behind the wheel. "They're nothing compared to my tongue."

Starting the car, he quickly backed out of his spot. "Forewarned is forearmed."

His confidence was both charming and annoying. She gave him the benefit of the doubt, knowing her hormones were bouncing around higher than kernels of corn popping in a microwave.

"Not hardly," she assured him.

Slade had a feeling it wasn't just an idle threat. Something told him that he would never really be forearmed around Sheila. But that was all right, too. That unknown element was part of the attraction.

Easing his foot onto the accelerator, Slade made it past the only light they would have to take before it turned red. The long, curving path onto the hospital grounds was just ahead on his right.

Slade realized that he'd undergone a change while overseas. This time around, his perspective on things had been altered. What had been important before no longer was. Conversely, he had a new set of values in place, a new set of goals.

During the last nine months, while death and destruction had left calling cards before and after his arrivals, at times existing side by side with him, Slade had realized that there were things he still hadn't done, things he *wanted* to do. Small, yet infinitely precious things. He didn't want to die before he did them.

He wanted to hold his baby in his arms, to make love to his wife. To wake up each morning with the same woman beside him.

Finding Sheila pregnant like this almost made it seem as if someone had been listening in on his thoughts and then had arranged his life for him accordingly.

Looking back, he realized that all that death, waste and devastation he had borne witness to had made him long to hang up his mantle as a disgruntled observer and live a little of his own life. To rejoice in the mundane things for a change.

To stop and smell the baby powder.

And now that it had actually happened, albeit completely without his knowledge and with no aforethought, Slade still didn't want to relinquish what he felt was a God-given mandate to go on with his life.

It wouldn't have been right. And he was a great believer in right.

The few spaces reserved for Admitting and Discharge were all filled. Muttering under his breath, Slade drove toward the general guest parking lot. He glanced at Sheila as he guided the car slowly around a wide curve.

"You owe it to the baby to give it a name." She opened her mouth with a rebuttal, but he was faster. "A proper name."

"Proper?" she echoed. Just what was he insinuating? "Have you bothered to look at the date on the newspapers carrying your articles? It's the nineties, Slade. People don't think that way anymore."

People hadn't changed all that much over the decades. They were still people. And old prejudices died hard. He didn't want any stigmas attached to his child.

"Don't they?" he prodded. "Don't you?" he added quietly.

They had done a lot of talking the night they met. Some of it, he knew, had been due to the wine, but some of it had been from the heart. For both of them. He felt he'd gotten to know her pretty well. This would matter to her, in time, even if she pretended that it didn't.

They'd both talked about not being tied down, about not becoming involved in relationships. It had all been very philosophical and entertaining at the time.

And empty, he now realized.

Something in her soul had spoken to his that night. And he had wanted to answer.

Slade had a gut feeling that this was why he had eluded sniper fire in Bosnia and survived the bombing in Beirut. To come home and be a father to this child he hadn't known was waiting for him. There was no other possible explanation for why he had been so uncommonly lucky.

Stubbornly, Sheila refused to give him an answer.

He continued as if he hadn't been expecting one. "It might look better to your patients if their doctor was married, now that she has a baby."

Now he was pontificating. The irritation she felt cut through the wall of pain that was closing in again. "All I owe to my patients is my expertise." She thought of Mallory. Of Nicole and Erin before her. "And maybe a shoulder to cry on once in a while."

One eye on her, he cruised down one aisle and up another, looking for a space. He was afraid to just let her out while he parked the car. Was everyone in Newport Beach at the hospital today?

"And what do you owe the baby?"

That was easy. "Love." She spat the word out, her breath wrenched from her again.

It looked as if there was a space in the next row. Slade hoped no one would beat him to it before he managed to reach it. "How about responsibility?"

She would have laughed if she had the strength. This from a man who swore he wanted nothing more than to be footloose. "By marrying you?"

She was in labor, he told himself. There was no reason to take offense at her tone. "What's wrong with me?"

"Nothing." And as a lover, he was perfect. But a marriage needed more than just a supremely qualified lover. Besides, at this point, she wasn't certain that she could measure up as a wife, or as a homemaker, either. Her mother hadn't. Why should she be any different? "But I really don't know what's right with you, either."

By nature, he always sought the easy way. "We'll explore each other after the ceremony."

The simple statement stunned her. "Garrett, there isn't going to be a ceremony."

The impossible had never confounded him. He always saw it as a challenge. "I can pull strings."

He was serious. And probably certifiable. "I'm not interested in any strings, unless they happen to be around your neck." She stared at Slade as he pulled into a narrow spot that just barely accommodated the car. "Slade, I don't believe in marriage."

Sure she did. She was just afraid. He couldn't say he blamed her. There was always that element of risk, but that was what made it intriguing.

"I do. Right after 'truth, justice and the American way,' and right before the Dodgers winning the pennant again." He unbuckled his seat belt and turned toward her. "C'mon, Doc. Where's your sense of adventure?"

Sheila clutched her stomach. The activity inside there was intensifying. "Busy at the moment. Slade, table the conversation and get me into the hospital. I'm not sure how much longer I have."

Slade hurried around the other side and opened the door for her. Before she could think to protest, he picked her up into his arms. Even pregnant, she didn't feel that heavy, he thought.

The significance that he was holding both his future wife and his child hit him, and he smiled as he began to walk toward the hospital entrance.

"What do you think you're doing?"

"We can make better time this way," he assured her.

The irony of the situation struck him. He'd always been good at negotiating and getting himself out of tight spots. This time, he wanted into one. "I don't want my son—"

Another time, she would have thought of this as hopelessly romantic. Right now, it was just hopeless.

"Or daughter," she added.

He took the correction in stride. "Or daughter, to carry the stigma I did."

He sounded so serious. "Stigma?"

He nodded, his eyes trained on the hospital electronic doors. "The word *bastard* is just as loaded with pain now as it was years ago, Sheila." His eyes shifted to her face. Did she understand what he was trying to say? "I don't want my kid hearing it. Having it ring in his ears long after the words have faded in the air. Knowing he was different. Knowing his father didn't care enough to stick by his mother and at least try to form a union."

He had her, he thought, he could see it. There was empathy in her eyes.

"It might all be well and good intellectually for you, but that doesn't make a hell of a whole lot of sense to a kid who wants a father around just to chase away the shadows."

Slade stopped momentarily as a car began to back out of its space. The driver leaned out and waved him on. Nodding, he continued walking. And persuading.

"I want to be there to chase away his shadows, Sheila. I want to be there for him. And for you." He smiled into her eyes. "We were good together."

"We had one night." Despite her valiant try, he was wearing her down. She could feel her resolve weakening quickly.

She still smelled good, he thought. Just the way she had that night. Just the way she did in his dreams.

"Yes, and look what we accomplished." He nodded at her stomach. "Think of what we could do with more time."

People were looking at them and smiling as he walked into the hospital with Sheila in his arms. A volunteer behind the information desk picked up her telephone and began tapping out an extension immediately.

"Go straight to Admitting," she told Slade, quickly waving them on. "They'll have a wheelchair waiting for you."

"Slade—"

The chapel was to their right. It was a small, narrow room. The fading afternoon light was piercing the slender stained glass window, casting blue-and-gold rainbows on the carpet.

Beckoning to her.

"Marry me, Sheila," he whispered into her ear. "Let's give this a try. If it doesn't work, we can always get divorced. But give this kid a fair head start. Let him have a mom and dad. A matched set."

This was insane, she thought. Completely insane. "Like salt-and-pepper shakers."

He grinned. He had her, he thought. "I'll be the salt, you be the pepper."

She would have thought he would have assigned the roles the other way around. "Why?"

His grin grew larger, warmer. "Because I liked the fire in your eyes that night."

His charm was reeling her in, just as it had that night. Momentarily devoid of pain, she felt almost tempted. "This is crazy."

He shrugged with a laugh. "Hey, the world's a little crazy. This is the sanest thing I've done in the last nine months."

Sheila ran her tongue along her upper lip. "If I say yes—"

Impulsively, he brought his lips down to hers, tracing the path of her tongue. Damn, but she had an impact on him. He didn't want to give her up.

Her head spinning, Sheila struggled to regain her breath. He had managed to affect her more deeply than the labor pains did.

"If I say yes," she repeated, her voice shaky, "I want you to know it's just temporary. Just to give the baby a name. As you said."

He followed the arrows that pointed out the way to Admitting. "All right, agreed. But even a TV set comes with a one-year warranty."

Maybe it was the labor pains she was having, but she didn't follow him. "Your point?"

"Give the marriage a year. If things don't work out for us by then, we'll get a divorce."

Divorce. It was a cold, hard, sobering word. What was she doing, even entertaining this harebrained idea? Was she crazy? She had to be.

Common sense reared its head above the pain. "I don't know—"

His eyes held hers for a moment as he turned the corner. "Think of the baby."

He had to be kidding. "I don't think I can think of anything else right now."

He could feel Sheila begin to stiffen in his arms. She was having another contraction, he thought. Feeling helpless, Slade looked toward the admitting desk. The woman was already hurrying toward them. Behind her, an orderly was pushing a wheelchair.

He kissed her forehead. "Hang on, Sheila."

She would get through this, she told herself. Everyone else had. "I've no intentions of giving birth in the lobby."

She'd misunderstood him. "I mean, until I can get Father Cullum."

"Dr. Pollack, hi, I'm Rosa." The beaming young woman greeted her warmly, clasping her hand. "Everything's all ready for you. Dr. Kelly's on his way."

She didn't want Kelly on his way, she wanted him here. Most of all, she wanted this over with.

The orderly was easing the wheelchair under Sheila. He looked at Slade. "Father Cullum's on the third floor. But Dr. Pollack's not going to die, she's just having a baby."

Slade laughed. "Not for last rites," he told the man. He looked at Sheila. "For the first ones."

They were both crazy. Sinking into the chair, Sheila waved Slade away. "Go ahead, find him. I'm not promising anything."

Slade was gone before the orderly had a chance to take her down the hall.

Chapter Four

"Father Cullum?"

Slade rapped once quickly on the door before looking into the room. The nurse in the hall on three had told him that the priest was either in room 324 or 236. Slade found him on the first try. So far, his luck was holding.

The slight, silver-haired man in black slacks and a long-sleeved black shirt looked up and then smiled. His blue eyes crinkled in recognition.

"Slade, how are you?"

"That all depends on you." Slade looked at the young man in the bed. The latter seemed to be in fairly good condition. "Mind if I steal him?" Not waiting for an answer, Slade hooked an arm around the priest and ushered him into the hall.

Father Jon Cullum had met Slade Garrett over a year ago. It had been in connection with a story about the troubles in Northern Ireland and reactions of people who had grown up there but had moved away. Slade had come for a religious and personal viewpoint from Father Cullum. Over the course of the interview the two had grown friendly. He'd earned the priest's admiration and respect.

"Is there something wrong, Slade?" Rather than just take him out in the hall, Slade was leading him toward the bank of elevators.

"I'll explain on the way." Reaching the elevator banks, Slade pressed the up button.

Father Cullum looked at him, bewildered. "On the way to what?"

Slade heard the bell ring in the distance. Impatient, he pressed the button again. "The fifth floor. And my wedding." He glanced at the man at his right. "Hopefully."

The elevator arrived, and Slade quickly pulled the priest into the car in his wake.

Father Cullum felt as if he was getting pulled into something more than just the elevator. "You're getting married?"

Slade pressed the button for the fifth floor. "If you do the honors."

"Would you run that by me slowly?"

"I fathered a child, Father." Slade grinned at the odd way the words fell together. "I didn't know it until half an hour ago. I want to do the right thing and marry the woman. She's here," he explained, "in this hospital." He blew out a breath, knowing how off-the-wall this had to sound. Yet he knew it was right to do this. It was instinct, not emotion, that led him. "About to deliver at any minute." His eyes searched the priest's light blue ones. Slade saw compassion there and understanding. "Will you do it, Father? Will you marry us?"

There normally were conferences to attend and banns to post before any of this could take place. Father Cullum knew his superiors would have said no immediately. But he liked to think of himself as being a little more progressive. He'd seen a great deal of what life could throw at a man, both here and in his native Ireland. A lot of it wasn't pretty, or easy. It had taught him that every rule had to be bent at least once.

Still, he knew it was his job to counsel and to be the voice of reason.

The doors opened on five and they walked out. Father Cullum stopped immediately before the visitors' lounge, turning toward Slade."

"Have you stopped to think, lad?" He wasn't going to insult Slade by expounding on the importance of marriages and the solemnity of the contract he was entering into. Father Cullum figured a man like Slade knew. But he still had to ask. "Do you know what you're getting yourself into?"

Slade knew, or thought he did. Hoped he did. He nodded. "Sometimes, Father, you just have to go with your gut."

A twinkle of a smile played on the priest's lips. "Yes, but it's the rest of you that's getting married, as well." He began to review the legal requirements. "I need papers, blood tests. A license."

Details. And in his experience, details could always be managed. "I can get all those." Slade glanced over the man's head toward where he assumed the delivery room was. "But not in time." It might even be too late as it was.

Father Cullum arched a snowy white brow. "You might have thought of that sooner—"

Slade dragged a hand impatiently through his hair. He had to convince the man. "There was nothing to think about. I didn't know."

"She didn't tell you?"

Slade shook his head. "Not a word. She's strong-willed and independent."

The priest laughed softly to himself. He thought of his sister Deirdre. Her temper had been as fiery as the color of her hair.

"I know what you mean. I had a sister like that. Drove us all crazy, God rest her soul. Not a day's gone by that I don't miss her since she's gone on to her reward."

Slade breathed a sigh of relief. The man understood. "Then you know exactly what I'm talking about. She's proud, Father, but I'm proud, too. Proud of the child we're going to have. A child I want born with my name as well as my genes." He laid a hand on the small man's arm, enforcing his request. "I could get the blood tests and the paperwork, Father. But it would be too late. The baby's being born now." He began shepherding the priest toward the nurse's station. "He needs my name now."

Slade could see by the man's expression that he had almost convinced the priest.

"Well," Father Cullum said slowly, "'tis highly irregular...."

Slade moved in for the kill. "We could, of course, technically marry ourselves, but I'd rather have you officiating." So would Father Cullum, Slade was willing to bet.

Father Cullum could just hear the monsignor now, admonishing him. But he could also hear the soft cry of the infant in question. A brand-new soul with needs. He raised his brow. "The paperwork—?"

Gotcha. "I'll handle it all retroactively," Slade promised. "There're people I can call." Everything could be handled. What he needed right now was someone who could perform the ceremony.

Father Cullum smiled. The cherubic expression made him almost look like a prototype for St. Nick, if he'd been about fifty pounds heavier.

"I've no doubt of that. I'm sure you know a great many people you could call." He sighed, surrendering. "Well, I suppose we could call this an emergency."

Slade leaped at the brass ring and snared it. "It is."

Father Cullum studied his face for a moment, making his own evaluations. "And the young woman, she's consenting?"

Slade thought that in the grand scheme of things, he could be forgiven if he twisted the words around in his favor. "She told me to go find you."

Father Cullum clapped a hand on Slade's shoulder. His voice was kindly, not judgmental, when he spoke. "'Twas different in my time. Young people married, then they had the baby, not the other way around."

The priest looked as if he were about to launch into a story. The moments were precious, and they were slipping away. Sheila could be in labor for hours, or she could be delivering right now.

"Father," Slade urged, "if you could hurry—?"

The older man laughed to himself, but he quickened his step. "I'm thinking that hurrying is what got you into this in the first place." He saw the apprehensive look entering Slade's eyes. This wasn't the time for sermons, even if he were given to them. "No." He held up his hand. "I won't moralize. I promise."

There was only one nurse at the nurses' station when they approached. The others were busy on the floor. She looked at them, obviously bewildered by the priest's appearance, as they hurried up to her.

"Quick," Slade said, hoping he wasn't too late, "where's Dr. Pollack?"

"Room 520." Dr. Pollack was a favorite among the nurses. The woman began to hurry behind Slade as the two men went toward the room she'd given them. "Is something wrong? No one told me that she needed a priest—"

Slade didn't want to waste any more time explaining the situation. "Just a precaution," he assured her, ushering the priest along.

The nurse stopped following, but her uncertainty mounted. "Um, friends are supposed to wait in the lounge." She pointed in the direction they had just come from.

"I'm not a friend," Slade replied, tossing the words over his shoulder. They'd all find out soon enough. He might as well start the ball rolling. "I'm the baby's father."

Slade didn't turn around to look at her, but he heard the sharp intake of breath that announced the nurse's response to the information.

Father Cullum hesitated at the closed door. He'd never been present at a birth before. "Do you think it's appropriate?"

This wasn't the time for niceties. "Definitely." His hand on the older man's arm, Slade ushered Father Cullum inside the room.

Sheila was lying in the narrow bed, a monitor standing beside her like a electronic sentry. She had her hands wrapped around the edges of the headboard. Every muscle in her body was rigid.

God, she looked awful, he thought. Tenderness, sweet and stinging, rose up within his chest as he approached the bed. "Sheila?"

She couldn't answer him. Not until her jailer set her free.

When the contraction was over, Sheila sagged against the mattress, visibly drenched. She'd stood on the other side of this so many times, watching the monitor foreshadow contractions, commiserating with her patients. But she had never had a real affinity for the scope of their pain. Not until this moment.

Sheila exhaled loudly, her breath shuddering through her body. She hadn't realized that she had closed her eyes until she opened them again.

She was glad to see Slade, glad to see someone here to hold the mounting fear at bay. She hadn't thought she'd feel that, either, but it was there, a tiny pygmy warrior pricking at her consciousness, making her afraid.

"Slade." She sighed his name, trying to catch her breath. "I thought you'd had a change of heart."

"Not a chance." He took her hand in his. "Father, this is Dr. Sheila Pollack." He looked down at her, a sense of wonder nudging at him. It was still so hard to believe. He was going to have a child. "The mother of my baby."

Making his way around the monitoring equipment, Father Cullum leaned over and politely took her hand in his. Hers was slick with perspiration. He gave her a comforting smile. "So, Slade tells me that you want to get married."

She wasn't so overcome with pain that she didn't want to set the record straight. Her eyes shifted toward Slade. "Slade wants to get married, Father."

Father Cullum sensed her embarrassment and detected a trace of reluctance. Though he wasn't the type to coerce, he fell back on the teachings he held dear. Still holding her hand, he reached for her soul and found the entrance through her eyes.

"A child deserves to be born with the advantage of having both parents in its life." The kindly smile widened. "Haven't you heard, Doctor? The family is making a comeback."

She smiled weakly, glancing toward Slade before answering the priest. "He's been talking to you, hasn't he?"

"Aye." Father Cullum nodded. "I have the bent ear to prove it. Now then, I take it that this is your wish, as well?"

It was framed in the form of a question, but it was clear that he was coaxing the right answer from her. Now that he was here, he was convinced that it was destiny that he should join these two together.

Sheila was tired, more tired than she'd ever been in her life, facing who knew how many more hours of labor. She had no strength to argue, and maybe, just maybe, Slade was making some kind of sense.

Besides, maybe somewhere deep down inside, she had never gotten over that night on the beach, or the man who had made time stand still for her.

"Yes." She hissed the response as another contraction began to take hold. It built up quickly until there was nothing but it and her. Everything else in the room disappeared.

Sheila clenched her jaw, desperately not wanting to cry out. The groan escaped nonetheless.

It prompted Father Cullum to open up his prayer book. He turned quickly to the proper passage, though it was out of habit rather than need. A priest for more than thirty years, he had married enough couples in his time to fill a good-size theater.

"Then I think that I had better do this quickly, my dear, and then get out of your way."

Slade took Sheila's hand in his. "The short version, Father," he urged. "Please." He felt Sheila's fingers tightening around his. Was she afraid, or was another contraction on the way? He glanced at the monitor's screen. There was no wave approaching. "Go ahead."

Father Cullum hoped the monsignor was going to be reasonable when he listened to this story.

"Do you, Sheila Pollack, take this man, Slade Garrett, as your lawfully wedded spouse, for better or for worse, in sickness and in health, to love and cherish as long as you both shall live?"

She twisted, knowing it was useless. The contraction was going to follow her everywhere on this narrow bed. And beyond. She spoke quickly, while she still had the breath to do so. "I do."

It was coming, Slade thought. He could see it on the screen. A wave that was growing larger and larger until it washed over Sheila, consuming her. Her fingers were digging into his. He held on, wishing that he could somehow fuse her pain into himself.

"And do you, Slade Garrett, take this woman, Sheila Pollack, as your lawfully wedded spouse—"

Oh my God, the baby's coming. She could feel it pushing. Sheila looked at Slade in panic. "I think it's coming!"

Father Cullum sped up, one word tripping after the next. "For better or for worse, in sickness and in health, to love and cherish as long as you both shall live?"

She arched into a sitting position, pulling herself on Slade's hand. "Oh, God, Slade, call the nurse. *Now.*"

"Not yet," he entreated her. "Hold on, Sheila, hold on. I do," he answered Father Cullum. Slade waved his hand to speed up the older man's words even faster. The other hand, clutched in Sheila's, was being crushed as she tried to ride out yet another contraction.

"By-the-power-vested-in-me-by-the-state-of-California-I-now-pronounce-you-man-and-wife." It came out as almost one word. Father Cullum shut his book and exhaled. "I usually say you may kiss the bride here, but it looks like you've already done far more than that."

Sheila whimpered, waiting for the pain to subside before she spoke. Her baby was fighting hard to emerge. "Slade—"

He didn't think that Sheila realized that she was still clutching his hand. He disengaged himself from his new wife. Adrenaline pumped through him, making everything appear just a little surrealistic. Just like it did during the events he'd covered as a journalist.

"I'm getting her," Slade promised.

Father Cullum was already slipping out. Slade caught up to him at the door. "Thanks, Father." Slade pulled out a wad of bills from his wallet.

Father Cullum began to decline. After all, these weren't exactly ordinary circumstances.

"For the parish," Slade urged, pushing the bills into the man's hand. Having done that, he pulled open the door and hurried into the hallway.

Father Cullum took the money and folded it into his prayer book. They could do with a few new hymn books, he thought.

"My congratulations," he said to Slade's back. "And don't forget to get the license to me so I can sign it properly."

"Will do," Slade called over his shoulder. The full impact of what he had just done hadn't hit him yet. There wasn't time. "Nurse!" Slade called. Alerted by the urgency in his voice, the young woman hurried over. "I think it's time."

She turned on her heel. "I'll get Dr. Kelly." After examining Sheila, the doctor had gone to look in on another patient on the floor.

"Thanks." Slade hurried into Sheila's room. He didn't want to leave her alone.

Married, he thought. They were married. He sincerely hoped he knew what he was doing.

One look at Sheila chased away any lingering doubts. She looked so vulnerable. She needed him, he thought. The baby needed him.

It was going to be all right.

He took her hand in his, holding tightly. "Dr. Kelly's coming."

Sheila felt as if she had almost bitten through her lower lip. In a haze of hot, demanding pain, she looked at Slade, moving her head from side to side. "Not soon enough." *Oh, God, here it comes again.* "Slade, get the nurse in here."

He jerked a thumb toward the hall. "But she's looking for— "

There wasn't any more time for talking. Holding on to the side rails, Sheila pulled herself up into a semisitting position, panting.

Slade stared at her. "What are you—?" She'd stopped panting and began straining. A guttural groan materialized from nowhere, even though her lips were closed. "My God, Sheila, you're having the baby."

Taking a break, she panted, her head falling back. "What was your first clue?"

So this was what it felt like. This was what her patients had all endured. It felt as if her entire body was being ripped apart.

At a loss, he pulled the side rail down to get closer to her. "What do you want me to do?"

"Hold my shoulders." Sheila braced herself to push again as Slade scrambled onto the bed behind her.

She was vaguely aware of the door opening and closing, and of people rushing in, surrounding the bed. She began panting, knowing intellectually that this would help, emotionally afraid that it wouldn't.

"God, Sheila, you're always in such a hurry." Dr. James Kelly, a tall, angular man, sighed, a smile playing on his lips. "When I examined you a few minutes ago, you were only at five."

She knew what she knew. Her eyes were almost wild as she looked up at the obstetrician. "I'm a ten, Jim. A ten."

Doing his best to put her at ease, Jim patted her hand. "I was speaking of the dilation," he teased.

Slade couldn't help wondering if there was more than just camaraderie between them. It was a stupid time to feel jealous, he thought. But it only further proved to him that he'd been right to do what he had.

"So am I." She didn't know if she could stand much more of this. "Slade?"

She needed to hold on to something, to someone. Sheila had no idea how lonely it felt to be pregnant like this. She'd borne up to it until now, but this last leg of the journey seemed so isolated to her. Knowing exactly what was waiting for her didn't help. It didn't cut through the loneliness or the fear.

Pain blocked her at every turn.

He would have held her to him if he could. "Right here,
Sheila. I'm right here." Slade raised his eyes to the doctor.
The man had the sheet back and was taking measure of just
how far along Sheila actually was. "What do you want me
to do?"

They had a moment, Jim thought, dropping the sheet
back into place. But just barely. He nodded to the nurse to
begin preparations in the delivery room. "For openers, you
might tell me who you are."

This was a hell of a time for introductions. "My husband," Sheila panted.

This was news to her colleague. "Boy, can you ever keep
a secret." They had covered for each other for three years
now. Jim thought he knew Sheila as well as anyone on the
staff did. Everyone had assumed that she had taken on the
role of a single mother. When had she gotten married?

He took careful measure of the man beside her. "All
right, Sheila's husband," Jim said gamely. "You'll find a
surgical shirt and pants to put on in the locker room. It's
right outside the delivery room." He smiled down at Sheila.
"We're going in, Sheila. Or rather, the baby is coming out."

Jim wasn't telling her anything she didn't already know.
"Hurry," Sheila breathed.

"We'll do our best. The rest is up to you." Jim was already out in the hall.

Her eyes turned toward Slade, stopping him from leaving. "Hell of a homecoming, isn't it?"

Slade wiped away the beads of perspiration along her
brow. Tenderness flowed through him, filling every available space in his body. Yeah, he thought, he'd done the right
thing.

"Can't say I'll ever forget it. I've been stateside for less
than twenty-four hours and I've gotten a wife and a baby.
Don't think I'll be able to top that any time soon."

He squeezed her hand, and then bent over, lightly touching his lips to hers. He saw the question in her eyes. "Now

it's official," he whispered, remembering the priest's words. "We're married."

She wasn't following him. "And if you didn't kiss me, we wouldn't be?"

He grinned, his eyes caressing her. "Nope."

He was a strange, strange man. "What if I didn't kiss back?"

"Too late. You did." He winked at her, squeezing her damp hand again. "See you in a couple of minutes, Mrs. Garrett." Slade hurried out.

Sheila had a feeling that it would have to be sooner than that.

"Rachel," she breathed, unable to find the nurse. It seemed ironic. How many times had Rachel assisted her as she brought a brand-new baby into the world? Now she was going to be assisting again, but there would be a new spin to the situation.

"Yes, Dr. Pollack."

It wasn't a question. Rachel understood what she was being asked to do. The nurse angled the gurney out into the hall. The delivery room was just two doors.

Sheila heard a woman screaming somewhere on the floor as they approached the delivery room. She winced in sympathy as another contraction rolled in.

She wasn't going to do that, she swore to herself. No matter how much she wanted to, she wasn't going to scream. "If I pull off your arm, Rachel," she said weakly, "I didn't mean it."

Rachel pushed the gurney into the delivery room. "I know that. You'll do fine."

Sheila tried to smile as Rachel lined up the gurney beside the delivery table. Her face didn't seem to be cooperating. "Funny, I've said the same words to I don't know how many patients. I wonder if they didn't believe me, either."

Rachel only laughed. "I'd wager that they all believed you. You're too good a doctor to lie." Gurney in place, she backed away. "I'll be right back."

Momentarily alone, Sheila stared at the huge light directly above her head. How many times had she been in this very room, on the other side of the stirrups? Seeing it from this angle put a whole new perspective on it. Had she been too blasé with her patients? Did they feel like hitting her when she was cheerful?

Mentally, she apologized to each and every one of them.

Slade, dressed in green livery, was suddenly beside her. He took her clenched hand in his. "It's going to be fine," he promised her.

Logically, she knew that. But it was hard to think with all this pain. "Easy for you to say."

"Yeah, it is," he agreed. "My stomach's upset, if that's any consolation."

She appreciated what he was trying to do. "You're just sorry you married me."

There she was dead wrong. "No, can't say that I am." He nodded at the doctor as the man walked in.

On his signal, the doctor, Rachel and another nurse moved Sheila from the gurney onto the delivery table. The nurse pushed the gurney aside as Rachel quickly slipped the white paper leggings onto Sheila before positioning her in the stirrups.

"Well," Jim announced, "we're all here. And you two have already been fruitful and multiplied." He chuckled at his own joke. "Let's see your work, Sheila." He glanced up at Slade who was positioned behind her. "On my count, support her shoulders. You know the drill, Sheila. One, two, three. Push."

Sheila was certain that she had ground her teeth to nubs as she screwed up her eyes, and her mouth, and pushed for all she was worth.

And then pushed again.

"Rest!" David ordered.

But she didn't. She couldn't. With all her heart, she knew that the baby had to emerge now. Now or never. She was light-headed and dizzy, but she continued bearing down and pushing.

Until it was over.

Falling back against Slade's arms, she gasped for air. The sound mingled with the lusty cry that filled the delivery room.

Bending, Slade brought his mouth down to her ear. "It's a girl," he whispered to her, his throat suddenly tightening to a pinhole. "We have a beautiful, pink baby girl."

His arms still around her shoulders, Slade couldn't remember ever being happier.

Chapter Five

Slade walked off the elevator into the newspaper office. Semicontrolled chaos was going on all around him, but for the first time that he could remember, he didn't feel as if he were part of it. He was preoccupied. And riding a high of a very unique nature.

He'd never pictured himself in a traditional role. Never once thought of himself as being someone's husband, much less someone's father. But he knew when a thing felt right. And this did. It felt good right down to the bone.

Though he wasn't aware of it at first, he couldn't help humming to himself.

Walking into his editor's office, Slade lifted the lid on the huge white box he was carrying and placed it in front of the man on his desk.

Andrew Wendell raised his eyes from the keyboard he had been pecking at. The cursor on the blue screen hovered between two paragraphs, blinking impatiently.

"Well, you look pretty pleased with yourself for a man who's a day late reporting in. Lucky for you your articles got here in time. Nice piece of work, Garrett. Welcome back." Doughnuts were a particular weakness for Andy, though no one would have ever known it to look at his rail-thin body. He eyed the box like a man who hadn't eaten in days. "What's the occasion?"

Slade pushed the box closer to him until it was almost under his elbow. "Have a doughnut, Andy. I just had a daughter."

Andy claimed a jelly doughnut while eyeing a second one covetously. "A daughter?" he echoed incredulously.

Munching, Andy scratched what was left of his faded rust-colored hair and stared at the man he had long since given up trying to pigeonhole. It had taken less than a month of working together for him to ascertain that Slade Garrett was one of a kind. And one was enough. But that one, he'd also found, was very essential to him.

"You been holding out on us?" Slade was known to have a strange sense of humor at times. It helped offset the sobriety of the events he covered. Was this his idea of a joke? "I didn't even know you were married. Or don't people like you do things like that anymore?"

Slade picked up the framed photograph on Andy's desk. It was a family portrait of Andy, his wife, who was a head taller than he was, and his daughters. All five of them. Studying it, Slade wondered what that would be like, to have five daughters. He wondered how Sheila felt about large families.

Boy, talk about a turnaround, he mused. He'd certainly done one in the past day.

He returned the photograph to its place. "Done. As of this afternoon."

It seemed as if all the hair Andy had lost had somehow found its way to other places on his face. His brows appeared to get thicker every year. He arched one now as he studied his best foreign correspondent while making short work of the doughnut. "Cutting it a little close, aren't you?"

That only added to the sense of excitement he felt. Slade grinned, making himself comfortable in the roomy, cracked upholstered chair by Andy's desk that he strongly suspected had once been part of the man's own collection at home before his wife had opted to redecorate.

He laid his ankle across his thigh. "When did you know me not to?"

That was what gave Slade an edge as a reporter. Andy nodded as he licked his red-stained fingers. A dot of red found its way to his shirt, and he muttered under his breath.

"That's the truth, all right." Finished, Andy didn't hesitate to select another one. "How come doughnuts? Aren't cigars still the tradition?"

Amused, Slade watched the man eat. Maybe he should have brought five dozen instead of four. He'd forgotten about Andy's tapeworm. It was either that, or he was harboring an alien inside of him. Andy could outeat anyone on the floor with no ill effects, no visible weight gain.

Slade shook his head in reply. "Not with the new no-smoking laws in the building. Besides, I don't want anything triggering me again." Not that he actually thought it would. Once he'd made up his mind about something, he stuck by it. And he'd made up his mind to stop smoking. "This time I've quit for keeps."

"Yeah, I can remember the promises I made with each new kid." Andy eyed the photograph on his desk as if he were really seeing it for the first time in a long while. "A daughter, eh?" He chuckled softly to himself as he shook his head. "Can't say I can picture you with anything under the age of eighteen bouncing on your knee."

"You're going to have to start." And so was he, Slade thought, steeping himself in the idea. Every time he thought of it, it was like opening up a huge Christmas present all over again. A Christmas present he hadn't even known was waiting for him. It added to the intensity of the rush he experienced at each interval.

"Welcome back, stranger. I heard you were here."

The words mingled with a rustle behind him and the scent of expensive perfume. Slade only had enough time to turn around before Laura Moore planted a friendly kiss on his mouth.

The hug he returned was quick and perfunctory. Laura was surprised at the lack of feeling she detected. Recovering nicely, she stepped back and glanced at the box on Andy's desk.

"Are we celebrating something?"

Andy rather than Slade pushed the box toward her. "Yeah, Garrett's descent into fatherhood." He eyed his gossip columnist for a reaction. They had a gossip mill of their own at the newspaper, and it had pegged Garrett and Moore as an item. "He's got himself a daughter. A wife, too."

Laura's eyes darted down to Slade's face a shade too quickly. It was true. She could see it. Amusement covered the sharp prick of disappointment she felt, at least for now.

"You're kidding." She selected a pink, heavily frosted, doughnut. At the moment, the calories didn't count.

He and Laura had shared some warm nights together, but it had all been more in friendship than anything else as far as he was concerned. Slade counted Laura among his friends. "Nope. It's your fault, really."

Her brows arched in genuine surprise. "This one you're going to have to explain to me."

Yes, Slade thought. It really was due to Laura that he'd met Sheila. And, apparently, his destiny, as well. "If I hadn't gone to cover for you at the fund-raiser at Harris Memorial just before I went on assignment, I would have never met her."

The doughnut didn't taste as good as it should. Her smile was spasmodic. "Just call me Cupid. What's her name?" Slipping into gear, Laura prodded for more information.

"Dr. Sheila Pollack." He'd married a doctor. He grinned to himself. That should make his mother happy. She had never expected him to marry anyone. Neither had he.

One favor and she was out of the running. Fate was really fickle sometimes, Laura thought with a pang.

The name was familiar to her. "Weren't her parents the ones spearheading the affair for the new obstetrics wing?"

Slade leaned over and took a doughnut himself. He hadn't eaten very much in the last twenty-four hours and it was catching up to him. "The same."

Laura blew out a breath, and with it, any residue of frustration that lingered. She knew how to roll with the punches.

"I asked you to cover the affair, not have an affair and cover the doctor," she reminded Slade with a wicked grin.

Their eyes held for a moment. Their times together had been good, Slade thought. But all that was in the past. He intended to do justice to his new role. And his new family.

"Water under the bridge, Laura." He had details to see to, Slade thought, rising. "I'll check in with you later," he promised Andy.

"He's off-limits now, Laura." Andy's voice was gentle, but firm.

Laura allowed herself one sigh as she watched Slade walk through the outer office. "He always was, Andy. He always was."

A splitting headache greeted her as Sheila opened her eyes. It didn't take any deep analysis to know that the pain had nothing to do with her physical condition and everything to do with her marital one.

The realization jumped up at her like an old-fashioned jack-in-the-box just as the last note was played.

Married.

She had married Slade. Somewhere in between gut-wrenching contractions, she had ground out the words "I do" to the questions of a wispy little man dressed in black, and had married Slade Garrett.

Had she lost her mind?

Pressing a hand to her forehead, Sheila sighed deeply. She couldn't even blame her impulsive action on the mind-clouding effects of drugs. She hadn't been given any medication. This colossal error she found herself in the middle of was nobody's fault but her own.

Hers and that silver-tongued journalist who had the capacity to unravel her the way no one else had ever even come close to doing.

She held her head in her hands. So what was she going to do now?

"How are you feeling, Dr. Pollack?"

Startled, Sheila looked up. She hadn't even heard anyone enter the room. With effort, she collected herself and forced a smile to her lips. She thought she recognized the young nurse, but wasn't certain.

"Groggy. Achy."

The nurse nodded. "Well, you know that's to be expected. I'm Alice," she told Sheila in case the doctor wanted to ring for her later. Competently, she took Sheila's vital signs and noted them on the chart clipped to the foot of the bed. Everything was on target. Finished, she smiled. "Would you like me to bring the baby to you?"

Her baby. She'd had a girl. Exactly what she'd hoped for.

Sheila nodded. "Please." She sat up higher in the bed, smoothing out her blanket. "Remind me why I went through all this in the first place."

Without another word, Alice left the room. She returned within a few minutes. Tiny mewling sounds were coming from the bundle in her arms. A maternal look entered her eyes as she held the infant to her for a moment longer.

"We took a survey on the floor." She beamed at Sheila. "Everyone thinks she's the prettiest baby in the nursery."

That made it unanimous, Sheila thought. She leaned forward to take the infant into her arms. As she felt the light weight, warmth flooded through her to such a degree, it startled her.

Hers.

Her own baby. It was hard to believe it was really true. She'd held so many others in her arms, yet this felt different. So very different. She wanted to do so much for this tiny being in her arms. Give her wings. Protect her.

Diametrically conflicting emotions bounced off one another in a flurry of confusion. She'd hoped she'd get it all straight by the time the baby graduated high school.

Sheila smiled knowingly at the nurse. "You have to say that."

Alice shook her head with feeling. "Oh, no, it's true. She is."

Sheila looked down at the tiny puckered face of her daughter and fell hopelessly in love all over again. Most babies had heads that were a little misshapen, but not hers. The perfectly shaped little head was fringed in dark brown hair. Dark brown, like Slade's, with eyes the color of the sky.

"Yes, I suppose it is. She is beautiful," Sheila whispered in awe.

Alice lingered a moment longer. For a change, there weren't many mothers on the floor, so she could afford to dawdle for a couple of minutes. "Do you have a name for her yet?"

A name. Sheila had thought of her tiny tenant as Baby for so long that she hadn't thought to select a name for her child. She'd been too busy, she thought ruefully, silently apologizing to the child in her arms.

"How about Rebecca?"

The deep male voice rumbled across her skin. Shaking off its effect, Sheila looked up to see Slade entering the room.

Six foot two, and all of it trouble, she thought, pressing her lips together. Married. She must have been crazy.

"Rebecca?" she repeated slowly, turning the name around on her tongue and in her mind as the nurse quietly withdrew from the room.

Slade came up to stand beside her and look down at his daughter. The sight had the effect of a one-two punch and brought him to his knees, humbled. Seeing her, he still couldn't quite believe it, even though he now had the license making it all legal in his pocket, awaiting Sheila's signature.

"It's my mother's name. I was always kind of partial to it."

"Rebecca," Sheila repeated again, looking down at her daughter. Trying it on for size. "Rebecca Susan." She added her own mother's name to the combination. "Such a big name for such a tiny thing."

Almost hesitantly, he reached over and touched the baby's clenched fist. Touching the miracle he had had a hand in creating. Just as in the delivery room, something tightened, swiftly and hard, within his stomach. He'd taken on adversaries of all kinds in the years he'd been a journalist. Lived through and seen things that would make the average man quake in his living room.

So how was it that something so small could reduce him to the consistency of warmed-over oatmeal?

"Becky Sue, then?" he suggested, looking at Sheila for approval.

"Becky Sue," Sheila echoed, unconsciously nodding. A smile curved her mouth as she tested out the sound. "Becky."

The baby made a noise that sounded very much like a squeak.

Sheila laughed to herself. Such a sweet sound, she thought. "Well, she likes it."

Slade nodded, as if he'd expected nothing else. Less than a day old and she already held him in the palm of her hand. "I guess it's unanimous, then."

Sheila raised a brow as she looked at Slade. The sight of his profile, so close, so compelling, reminded her how she had gotten into this situation in the first place. "Don't I get a vote?"

He knew he could pull up a chair, but somehow, that didn't seem close enough. Slade remained where he was, standing beside Sheila and the baby, absorbing the sensations the proximity created. He shrugged in reply to her questions.

"This is classic democracy at work, Sheila. 'Rebecca' wins, two to one." He placed a hand on her shoulder. "But you can still come in on the winning side if you like."

"Thanks a lot." She laughed as she shook her head and looked at the baby. Rebecca Susan. She liked the sound of that. But she couldn't just agree. He wouldn't expect it of her. "You just steamroll over everything, just like in your articles, don't you."

Slade looked at her, surprised and pleased. "You've read my articles?"

Sheila shrugged, reaching for nonchalance to cover the sudden self-consciousness she felt. "A few. I was just curious what you sounded like on paper."

She didn't want to admit that reading the articles had managed to hearten her. That though she'd had no intentions of getting in contact with him about the pending blessed event, reading his words, seeing events through his eyes, had somehow made her feel closer to him. And be proud of the conviction and power she found there. And she'd even started a small scrapbook of his articles for the baby, to tell her about her father when the time came.

It had helped.

He crossed his arms before him. "So, what did you think of my work?" He knew better than to expect flattery, but that wasn't what he was after. He genuinely wanted to know what she thought.

His articles had been compassionately vivid, bringing the scenes he witnessed into her life. But telling him that seemed in the nature of pandering. It didn't fit the fledgling relationship they had. Sheila smiled at Rebecca, who was now trying to eat her fist, and raised her eyes to his. "This is the best example."

If she was expecting a display of ego, Slade thought, she was going to be disappointed. He'd already reached that conclusion himself. "No argument."

His answer had her softening a little and brought them closer to the same side. Without realizing it, she'd placed them on opposite ends of the court, opponents, though she couldn't have stated what they were on opposite sides about if she were asked. It was just the way she'd viewed him and their situation.

Sheila sighed and shook her head. "This is highly unorthodox, you realize."

"Sheila—" Slade made himself comfortable on the corner of her bed as he faced her "—I've been in and out of so many places, places that suddenly became new countries overnight, seen people who had everything when they went to sleep the night before wake up to total poverty, watched once-picturesque spots become blighted with bodies and blood. I don't think I really know what 'unorthodox' is anymore."

She didn't have his frame of reference, she had only her own. Except for that one night, her life had been led on the straight and narrow.

She held her infant daughter close to her heart and looked up at the child's father. "This is it, trust me."

Impulsively, he leaned forward and cupped the back of her head. As the very breath stopped within her lungs, Slade brought his mouth down to hers.

The kiss began like a whisper of a song on her lips. His whisper. It grew until the song became a symphony that enveloped her, taking her out of the normal trappings of her life and putting her in a place only lovers visited.

If they were very, very lucky.

It took her a moment to get the room to stop spinning. Dazed, she looked at him for an explanation. "What was that for?"

He built on the word she'd used. "I trust only what I can see and touch." And besides, he'd wanted to do that for the last nine months. That and more. But more, he knew, was going to have to wait.

She swallowed, wondering why her heart thudding against her rib cage wasn't startling the baby. "And kiss, obviously."

His smile was the most sensual one she'd ever seen. "We all have our own way of touching."

She had to keep her mind, what was left of it, at any rate, on what she wanted to say to him. "I wasn't in my right mind yesterday—"

He didn't want to hear about any regrets. Not until he'd had an opportunity to erase them for her. "I was," he interjected mildly.

They weren't two teenagers who'd gotten drunk and driven over the border to Mexico for a quickie wedding. They were two professionals who had somehow managed to get a quickie wedding in the middle of the hospital. It was too bizarre for words.

Unable to put it into anything that might sound vaguely coherent, she stared at him. He *looked* sane, but she had her doubts.

"Are you trying to tell me you still want to go through with this?"

The grin only broadened, telling her she was right. "How am I doing?"

Why was it every time she was around him, she did irrational things? "Slade, this might be hopelessly romantic—"

Slade cut her short. "I see it as practical," he contradicted her. Her brows went up so high, they disappeared beneath her bangs. "We hit it off." He touched Rebecca's hand. "We created a child—"

She'd always maintained that accidents weren't necessarily the precursors of life sentences. "That doesn't mean we have to spend the rest of our lives together."

"Just the rest of our lives?" He managed to maintain a straight face. "I don't make commitments easily. When I do, they stick. I was thinking along the lines of eternity." His eyes teased hers, and she couldn't tell if he was serious or just having fun at her expense. "I figure you'll look pretty good with wings."

All she could manage in her defense was to recite an old adage. "Marry in haste, repent at leisure."

He shrugged away the prediction. "In my line of work, there's very little leisure."

Did he work at this charm, or did it just come naturally to him? "You said I had a year." It would have almost sounded like a prison sentence, if she didn't react the way she did to the warden.

Slade nodded. It shouldn't take him that long to convince her that they'd done the right thing. "You do—use it."

His gaze lingered over her. The blue nightgown, which was definitely not hospital issue, had slid off her shoulder, and he restrained the desire to touch her skin again. But soon, very soon, he promised himself.

"Or are you afraid that you might get to like the idea?"

She drew upon the way she'd always felt about marriage. It was a prison that locked people in, that made them unhappy. There was no other possible explanation why her parents spent so little time together. "It's not an idea, it's an institution—"

This was something they hadn't discussed that night. She had some very sad ideas about marriage that he felt an obligation to correct.

He toyed with her hair. "Institutions are where they put people away. I've no intentions of putting you away, Sheila." His voice grew serious. "You can live your life the way you want to. I don't want to change anything about you," he told her honestly. And then his mouth curved. "Just no dating."

Just when he was reeling her in, he cut bait. "Slade, be serious—"

Framing her face in his hands, he kissed her again, hinting at the passion that lay ahead of them. Passion she had been introduced to once before. Releasing her, he stepped back.

"I'm on my honeymoon, Doc. I don't have to be serious until I get back to work. Oh, I almost forgot."

As she watched him, her curiosity building, Slade stepped out into the hall. He returned a moment later with what he'd purposely left outside her room. He had wanted to see her unencumbered. Now he brought in a huge basket filled with a profusion of roses in different colors. Under his arm he carried an equally huge pink rabbit with enormous floppy ears.

Sheila stared at the bounty and felt herself smiling despite all her efforts not to. Damn it, now he was being sweet on top of everything else. He didn't play fair. "Who *are* you?"

Placing the basket on a side table and setting the rabbit on the chair, Slade squared his shoulders and started to recite, "Slade Garrett, social security number 170—"

Sheila held up a hand. This was cute, but it wasn't what she'd meant.

"I mean really," she said seriously. "I don't know anything about you except that you write for the *Times* and that you're a bastard."

Amusement danced in his eyes. "You're not talking entirely about parentage, are you?"

An equal dose of humor entered hers. "No, not entirely."

He was looking forward to swapping childhood stories with her. He had a feeling that hers were not as laid-back as she might believe. "We have the rest of our lives to find out—or a year, depending on whether or not you want to make use of your option clause."

She couldn't begin to figure him out. "You're serious? About the year?"

He took the baby from her arms. God, there was nothing like this feeling in the whole world. He glanced up at Sheila. "I'm serious about making you forget about the option in a year, but yes, at the end, if you don't think it'll work out, I'll agree to a divorce."

It didn't make any sense. Why bother in the first place? Why go through all this trouble? "Why are you doing this?"

"I already told you. I don't want the baby to feel like a—"

They'd been through that. It was what won her over. And yet, she couldn't help thinking there was something more. "Is that the only reason?"

"No," he said softly as he looked at her over their baby's downy head. "When I was overseas, I held on to a picture of you. It was the only thing that kept me going at times."

For a moment, she didn't know what to say. He was serious, she thought. Really serious. "I didn't give you a picture."

"Here." Holding the baby in one arm, Slade tapped his temple. "I had a picture right here. When the rebels overran the camp and the tent I'd been sleeping in five minutes earlier went up like a torch, my whole life didn't pass before my eyes. But that one night did. Our night." He blew out a breath. The image still left him numb. "I decided I had to see you again." He smiled, remembering his surprise at her condition. "And then I decided that I wanted to keep on seeing you. So it was either getting pregnant myself and availing myself of your services, or marrying you." He shrugged as he tucked the blanket more firmly around the baby. "I chose the easier way."

She thought of her parents. They were both such good people, just not good together. "You may not think so after a while."

"Why?" Very carefully, he laid the baby back into her arms. "What are you afraid of?"

If he was being honest, so could she. "I don't like failing, Slade."

There was a simple-enough solution to that. "Then don't."

She laughed dryly. "Not that simple."

"Not that hard," he countered. "I've always found that I can pretty much do what I set my mind to. Judging from your success, you do, too."

His answer surprised her. Had he had her investigated? "What do you know about me?"

He liked the way her eyes grew huge when she was caught unsuspecting. "You'd be surprised, Sheila. I'm not a man without connections."

Her brows drew together. She was right. "You had me investigated?"

He wouldn't exactly call it that, but why quibble over semantics? "It helped pass the time away."

She didn't understand. "But you were overseas all these months."

He nodded. "Yeah, but my connections are over here." And he had wanted to know things about her. So many things.

All this time, she had assumed that was nothing more than a pleasant memory to him. A one-time, one-night fling. "Seems to me you went to an awful lot of trouble."

"That's not how I see it." He looked down at his daughter. Rebecca was rooting. "I think she's hungry. Either that, or she sucked on a lemon." Without waiting, he turned and pulled the curtain in front of her bed, cutting off her view of the hall.

"What are you doing?"

"Giving you some privacy in case someone walks in while you're nursing Becky." He nodded toward the baby. "You are nursing, aren't you?"

She felt rosy warmth creeping up her neck and surprised herself. She hadn't thought she could blush. "That's rather personal, don't you think?"

"That's why I pulled the curtain." He paused, dropping the brashness like a second skin. "Which side of the curtain do you want me to stand on, Sheila?"

She would have said outside, but he had given her a choice, and in giving it to her, had turned the situation in his favor. As he probably meant to, she thought. The man was nothing if not clever, she thought with grudging admiration.

"You can stay here."

He smiled at her and nodded, sitting down again on the edge of the bed. "Thanks, I'd like that."

Chapter Six

Slade was accustomed to taking in his surroundings and evaluating them quickly. The decor in Sheila's two-story condominium was understated and tasteful. It spoke of class, not glitz. A little like, he thought, the lady herself.

"Nice place you have here," he murmured.

Setting the suitcase one of her nurses had brought her in the hospital down inside the living room, Slade closed the door behind Sheila. He arranged the stuffed rabbit on the first available surface, the sofa. It sagged forward, coming to rest against the coffee table as Slade turned toward her.

"Here," he coaxed, hands outstretched, "let me take her."

Before Sheila could demur, Slade had taken his daughter into his arms. The baby made a noise that he interpreted as a sound of welcome. At least, it would do for now.

"Hi, Becky. So, how'd you like your very first car ride?"

Baby in his arms, Slade moved around the living room as if to introduce Rebecca to it. There were built-in shelves on both sides of the white brick fireplace. The array of books pointed to eclectic taste. He and Sheila had that in common, he mused.

"Play your cards right, kid," he continued, "and I'll get you a red Corvette for your sixteenth birthday."

He was really taking to this, Sheila thought, watching him. She had no frame of reference as far as Slade was concerned, but she knew disinterest when she saw it and there wasn't a hint of it in his attitude. She never would have thought, looking at him, that he had a marshmallow center. She smiled as she shook her head.

"You're lucky she won't remember that."

"Why?" He looked up at Sheila. "I mean it. Everyone should have something to look forward to." He looked to his daughter for corroboration. "Right Becky?"

She refrained from taking her daughter back. After all, Slade deserved some time with her, too. She marveled that he even knew how to hold a baby.

"Right now," she said, "I think all she wants is to be fed and dry." He grinned at her. "What?"

"Sounds like my wish list when I was in Somalia." He thought about it for a moment. "And Bosnia. And—"

He was talking as casually about these places as if they were merely different stores located in the mall, or as if as if he were ticking off a list of amusement parks that littered the Southern California terrain, not the centers of death and annihilation. How could he remain so unaffected by them?

Or was that just a defense mechanism he used to keep himself sane?

"They sent you to all those dangerous places?" she asked incredulously.

He shrugged as he lost himself in Rebecca's smile. Some might have thought of it as a reaction to a gas bubble, but he knew better. It was his daughter's smile, and it was meant just for him.

I'll do right by you, little girl. I swear I will.

"It's where the news is," he answered Sheila.

Sheila nodded, saying nothing further. If she were really emotionally involved with him, the thought of his risking his life to get a story would have undone her. But she wasn't emotionally involved, she told herself.

The trouble was, she really didn't know what she was. This was very shaky ground she found herself on, and she didn't want to make any plans—or let any emotions make plans for her. She'd led with her emotions only twice. The last time she had gotten an eight-pound, three-ounce reward. The next time, she might not be so lucky.

She looked pensive, Slade thought. *Probably afraid that I might drop the baby.* He was about to offer Rebecca back to her when he heard someone entering the room behind him. He'd thought they were alone.

"Oh, Doctor, you are here. I am so sorry. I am not ready yet for you."

Slade turned around to see a slender young woman with long, straight blond hair hurrying into the room. Nurse? Housekeeper? He wondered if the woman lived in. Whatever the circumstances, he could adjust. Hell, he'd lived with five men in a ditch for what seemed like forever and shared the mouth of a cave with a family of refugees for a week. Sharing a house with two-and-a-half women was going to be no hardship.

He raised a brow as he turned toward Sheila. "And this would be—?"

Sheila moved to the young woman's side, placing her hand on the latter's shoulder.

It was a protective gesture, Slade noted, whether she knew it or not. Did she think the young woman needed protecting from him? The idea amused him. And maybe bothered him just a little.

"Ingrid Swenson, my cleaning lady's daughter," Sheila said. She smiled at the bewildered look on the younger woman's face. "Ingrid's going to help me with the baby. She's a student at UCI."

Students studied. When they didn't party, he thought. And Ingrid looked as if she would be a gorgeous addition to any campus party. "Then how—?"

"Night classes," Sheila answered, anticipating Slade's question. "It's just a temporary arrangement until I can interview a live-in nanny." The interviews were something she wasn't looking forward to. Part of her would have almost rather just remained home and been a full-time mother.

She'd be restless within two weeks, Sheila admonished herself. She wasn't the type who could really stay home, content in making baby food from scratch, doing fun things with papier-mâché and whipping up four-course meals.

"Oh, Dr. Pollack, she is beautiful," Ingrid cried, looking at the infant in Slade's arms. "May I please hold her?"

"That's the general idea," Sheila laughed. "You might as well start right in."

She had an affinity for this, Sheila thought, watching Ingrid as she took the baby from Slade. She knew exactly how to hold Rebecca, and there was pleasure in her eyes. Too bad the search couldn't end here, Sheila mused. Ingrid would be perfect for the position as nanny.

"I helped raise my four brothers and sisters," Ingrid told them. This arrangement meant a great deal to her, allowing her to pay for her schooling. She was grateful to the doctor.

Ingrid cooed at the baby. "But not a one of them was as angelic as this one." She looked up at Sheila. "What is she called, please?"

"Rebecca," Sheila said. "Rebecca Susan."

She took a deep breath. When she'd made arrangements for Ingrid to come stay with her and take care of the baby, she'd been a single mother. All that had changed since the last time she'd spoken with Ingrid. Sheila hadn't told anyone about her new change in status. She hadn't had to. Word about the bizarre wedding ceremony in the labor room had spread at the hospital like a prairie fire over dry grass.

She felt as if she was about to drop a bombshell. Ingrid, and especially Ingrid's mother, were old-fashioned people with solid values ground in tradition. She doubted if any of their ancestors had gotten married two minutes before delivery.

Unconsciously, Sheila licked her lower lip. "Ingrid, this is my husband, Slade Garrett."

Confusion entered the pale blue eyes as she cradled the baby against her. This was unexpected. "Mother did not tell me that you were married."

"Mother did not know," Sheila interjected. A smile quirked her mouth as she looked at Slade. She'd really gotten herself into something this time, she thought. But somehow, the accompanying tinge of regret was fading away to almost nothing. "Mr. Garrett is the old-fashioned type. He believes in issuing each child the standard mommy and daddy at birth."

"There's nothing standard about you," Slade quipped, giving Sheila a quick kiss. He paused, waiting. "Well?"

He'd lost her. "Well?" Sheila echoed, confused. "Well, what?"

"You're supposed to say the same thing back." He liked teasing her, he thought. Of course, he liked nibbling on her lower lip better, but you took what you could get. He was looking forward to the latter when the opportunity presented itself.

"The same thing back," Sheila parroted, smiling prettily like a cardboard debutante. He wasn't getting anything out of her until she'd made up her mind to give it.

Sheila sighed, surprised at how tired she actually felt. She'd always been able to go for more than twenty-four hours straight and still operate. It was a holdover from her medical student and resident days. But right now, she probably could have been knocked down by the proverbial feather.

"I think I'd like to change and put my feet up awhile," she told him.

Slade nodded, already making himself at home. "Fine. Do you need anything?"

A reality check would be nice.

What was she doing, playing house with a man she hardly knew?

Hardly knew but found devastatingly attractive, a perverse little voice within her whispered.

This definitely went against everything she thought she wanted for herself. She had made her choices years ago. A career, that had been her goal. Her only goal after her one disastrous foray into romance. She wanted a career being the best possible doctor she could be. Finding herself pregnant despite precautions, she'd adjusted so that she could assimilate a baby into her life and still try to make things work.

But a husband? Talk about a monkey wrench in the works, this was a biggie. Where did she get off thinking that this had a chance of working, too? Her mother and father hadn't been able to manage it, sailing through life like two polite, intelligent strangers adrift down the same river.

This hadn't a chance in hell.

Sheila shook her head a little too emphatically. "No, I'm fine."

No, she wasn't, he thought, but she would be. "Good, then I'm going to go and get some of my things out of storage and bring them over."

He was moving in. He was actually going to do it. A wave of panic rose up, clogging her throat. "Your things? What things?"

"Not furniture," he assured her. Furniture had never been a priority for him. He used what others thrusted upon him, except for his entertainment center, which he considered vital to his work when he was stateside. That had been first-rate. "I sublet my apartment. Besides, nothing that I have would fit in here. I'm just bringing some clothes, books and my camera equipment." The rest could be brought over later, he decided.

Her mouth felt cottony. Slade was moving in. He was really moving in. It was happening.

Panic buttons began depressing all through her, going into gear like inhabitants of a town perched at the base of an active volcano reacting to a sudden red glare lighting up the night sky.

"Want me to get anything at the store on my way back?" Slade asked at the door. "Something to celebrate our nuptials?" His mouth curved into a grin, but his eyes were serious.

She'd been too unsettled to eat this morning, she remembered. Her stomach felt as if it was tightening, but whether in hunger or in reaction to the moment, she wasn't certain.

This was a mistake, a big mistake, she thought. And yet, she couldn't help hoping that it wasn't.

"The gooeyest coffee cake you can find."

That sounded good to him. "I thought you were supposed to have cravings while you were pregnant, not afterward."

She shrugged, avoiding his eyes. "I never had the time."

"One gooey coffee cake coming up. See you in a couple of hours."

Slade bent to kiss her before leaving. Sheila turned her cheek toward him at the last moment. He brushed his lips over it and withdrew.

Maybe this was going to be slower going than he'd supposed.

It took him longer than he promised, and Sheila found herself watching the clock. It was a new experience for her. Impatience wasn't something she was acquainted with. The reverse was usually true.

Waiting for Slade to return was like waiting for the other shoe to fall.

Or the music to begin.

When she heard the doorbell, a sound she'd been waiting for for the last eighty-three minutes, it startled her. She saw Ingrid peer out of the kitchen and waved her back to whatever she was doing.

"I'll get it."

"But you should be in bed," Ingrid reminded her.

A thought, no doubt, that probably occurred to Slade, as well. And to her when she looked at him. "I will be. Later."

She opened the door just as he rang again.

She looked happy to see him. Or relieved, he thought. "Miss me?"

"Missed the coffee cake" was all she would admit to. She took the plastic grocery bag from him. It hung suspended from his fingertips. The rest of his hands and arms were occupied and filled to capacity.

He realized that she hadn't shown him where the bedroom was. "So, where do you want me to put all this?"

"All this" consisted of a handful of shirts and slacks and two boxes filled with miscellaneous paraphernalia he considered utterly indispensable. All but a little black book. That he'd bequeathed to the man subletting his apartment.

Sheila eyed the boxes uneasily. Try as she might, she couldn't picture him here, amid her tidy porcelain statues of people from another era. He seemed too rough around the edges.

That was what had made him so exciting to begin with, she reminded herself. He didn't belong in her world.

But he was in it now, all six foot two of him. "How much more is there?"

He didn't believe in a lot of baggage, but what he had was essential. He raised the boxes slightly to emphasize his point.

"This is it, except for the camera equipment. You learn how to make do with very little when you're on the move. When you find yourself stationary, it's hard to change old habits."

That's just what she was afraid of. Afraid that what they had brought into this hasty marriage were two people who were, at final analysis, as different from each other as the sun and a lantern. She was opting for the part of the sun.

She gestured that he should set the boxes down on the coffee table for the time being. She had something more immediate to attend to. The coffee cake. "Sounds like something printed on a dish towel belonging to someone on the run."

He wondered if she was trying to bait him into an argument and why. "At times, that's how I felt." Depositing the boxes on the table, he slipped his arm around her, preventing Sheila and the coffee cake from making a quick getaway.

"I was running from things then. Had I known about the baby..." He paused.

Her eyes held his. "What? If you'd known about the baby, you would have what?"

Slade shrugged. There was no use lying about the man he'd been. "Maybe I would have still run from, not to," he admitted.

He used the past tense. The cake could wait. "What changed your mind?"

"Seeing you again." He took the cake from her, setting it on top of the boxes, and hushed her fledgling protest with the tip of his finger. As she stared at him, intrigued, he slipped his hands around her waist and drew her closer. "When I did, suddenly, I knew everything that was missing in my life. We made a connection that night, Sheila, one that lasted, that went clear down to the bone. I'm not much good with words on a personal level—"

Did he really believe that? "You're doing well so far."

He continued as if she hadn't spoken. "But making love with you went beyond excitement. There was a certain peace to it." He was telling her more than he had ever told another woman. Because she made him feel more than any other woman ever had. "A peace I hadn't found yet. A peace that I haven't felt since I left you."

For someone who professed to have difficulty saying what was on his mind, he was very good. Too good. She couldn't help being just a shade suspicious. "And the guns and bombs going off didn't have anything to do with that?"

He looked at her seriously. "No, they didn't." He ran his hand along her arm. There was no reason why she should find it an immensely comforting gesture, but she did. "I'm not saying that this is going to be easy—"

Well, at least he wasn't trying to snow her. "If you did, I'd tell you about the mental health program that Harris Memorial is sponsoring." Pressing her lips together, she shook her head. "I still might." And there would be room for both of them in that program.

"But we can make it work," he assured her. "I want it to work." He'd never meant anything so much in his life. Slade lowered his mouth to hers, claiming the kiss she'd withheld earlier.

His lips moved over hers, coaxing them apart, deepening the kiss not by degrees, but like a flash point of a fire, burning a trail through her so quickly, she had no time to think, to save herself.

The kiss singed her, melted her until she barely had enough strength to stand. Sheila dug her hands into Slade's shirt, twisting it, just as the fire twisted within her.

If he meant to convince her, he more than ably convinced himself. Anything could work if you wanted it to, if you believed strongly enough that it would.

Unable to help himself, he slipped his hands beneath her blouse, wanting only to touch her skin, to touch and fantasize. And remember.

He cupped his hands gently along her breasts, exciting them both.

She tasted like sin, just as she did that night. Just as he knew she always would. Sweet sin. And his eternal undoing.

Blood rushing through his veins, emotions demanding release, he reluctantly drew his mouth from hers. It took him a moment to catch his breath.

"So, how about you?"

Every thought in her head was either scrambled or fried. She looked at him, dazed, disoriented. "What?"

"I said, I really want this marriage to work, how about you?"

Right now, he could have gotten her to swear allegiance to a cult that shaved their heads, wore goat skins and lived on the side of a mountaintop in Tibet. "Yeah, me, too."

Wedging a hand between them on his chest, his very hard, firm chest, she created a pocket of air. And a tiny space in which to attempt to gather her scattered thoughts together. She looked at him.

Maybe...

"But you're going to have to give me a little time," Sheila qualified slowly. "This isn't what I thought I ever wanted."

She'd never played house, never dreamed of being swept off her feet. She thought she'd seen through the hoax and had faced reality at an early age. There were no happily-ever-afters possible for someone dedicated to a career. And she was.

If she thought she had been initially wrong, there was Edward to remind her.

She didn't want to think about that now. This just might be different.

Maybe...

Slade left his hands on her hips a moment longer and pressed a kiss to her temple. "The best surprises are usually the unexpected ones. Like our daughter."

Our daughter. It had a hell of a ring to it, she thought.

She cocked her head. "Speaking of whom, I think I hear her crying."

If he listened, he could hear the tiny wail drifting down through the open nursery room door. "She probably wants to know where her father went."

Sheila cast one longing glance at the coffee cake. It would have to wait. "More than likely, where her dinner went."

His glance slid along her breasts, making her warm all over again. "Talking to her father." Slade picked up the box. "So, where's your bedroom? I want to stash this for the time being."

On her way to the stairs, Sheila stopped and looked at his belongings. "My room?"

"Well, you don't expect me to sleep with Ingrid, do you?"

She bit her lip. She hadn't thought about giving up her privacy. It seemed that there was a lot she hadn't thought about when she had ground out the words "I do." "No, I just hadn't thought—"

Slade was intrigued by her reluctance. "Didn't your parents sleep together?"

The smile on her lips had very little humor behind it. "They were hardly ever home at the same time for me to notice." With a sigh, she led the way upstairs.

Slade followed. "Trust me, married people sleep together. I have it on the best authority."

Sheila stopped in front of the nursery. "It's on the right." She pointed to the last room on the floor.

Sheila watched as Slade backed his way into the room. Her room. Their room. This was going to take *some* getting used to, she thought, walking into the nursery.

He'd stayed up, watching the news on her television set in the bedroom. It was past eleven before she drifted into the bedroom. The blue satin nightgown brought out her eyes. And his desire. With effort, he banked it down.

Exhaustion was etched into her face. He'd thought that Ingrid was supposed to take some of the burden off her shoulders, especially the first night. But knowing Sheila, she probably hadn't allowed it.

Knowing Sheila. He liked the sound of that. He planned to make it part of his life's work.

Slade clicked off the television set and laid the remote on the nightstand. "You look tired."

She didn't answer at first. Words took effort, and she had very little energy left to exert. "I am."

He patted the space beside him. "Then why don't you lie down?"

This was a hell of a time to suddenly feel shy. That should have happened nine months ago, on the beach, not here in her own bedroom.

Their bedroom, she corrected herself. "Um—"

Slade rose and crossed to her. Taking her by the hand, he led Sheila over to the bed.

"Lie down," he repeated, his voice soft, but stern. "I have no intentions of knowing you in the biblical sense until you get your own doctor's okay." His eyes held hers. "And you give me yours." His mouth softened into a smile. "I'm a nice guy, remember?"

Without thinking, she cupped his cheek. "You know, there's not that much to remember." With a sigh, she sank down onto the mattress.

"Oh, I don't know." Sitting down behind her, Slade began kneading her shoulders. There were knots the size of small boulders there. "I remember a lot. Played it over in my mind in slow motion at times. Like after we went swimming in the cove."

In hindsight, that had been an incredibly stupid thing to do. But it had felt so right at the time. "If someone had come and found us—"

"But they didn't," he reminded her. And that was all that counted. "Tell me, except for that night, are you always cautious?"

She began to turn to look at him, but he forced her back around. God, but his hands felt wonderful. "If you mean do I go skinny-dipping in the moonlight with just anyone, no, I don't."

"Just with me."

She could hear the smile in his voice. "Just with you."

"I like that." Still massaging her, he pressed a quick kiss to the side of her neck and felt her shiver in response. He hoped that would never change. "I like that a lot."

Sheila felt her heart racing. Exhausted beyond words, she could feel herself becoming aroused. There wasn't anything she could do about it yet. "Male ego?"

"Husbandly pride," he corrected her. He waited a beat. "And maybe a touch of male ego." He began to work her shoulders a little harder. "God, woman, you're as tense as an ironing board. Relax. You're home."

It wasn't that simple. She was home, all right, but with a whole new set of ramifications. "With a newborn depending on me."

"On us," Slade corrected her. "Depending on us. I'm here for the long haul, Sheila. I already told you that." He wondered how long it would take her to believe that.

She could see Slade reflected in the dark TV screen, looking a little larger than life. That's what he was, a little larger than life. And it scared her.

"You know," she said carefully, "I was always taught that if something looked too good to be true, it usually was."

Yeah, so was he. But every rule had an exception. And she was his. "What else were you taught?"

Sheila laughed softly to herself at the irony of it. "Not to be impulsive."

He grinned at the back of her head. "Glad you didn't take that one to heart."

She twisted around to look at him. "But I did. I do."

She had an image of herself as being straitlaced, but he knew better. "Is that why you made love with me that night, because you're not impulsive?"

She took a deep breath, intending on setting him straight. "I made love with you—"

He was the picture of innocence as he sat back on his heels. "Yes—?"

She'd never thought about it, actually, but she did now. And rattled off the reasons that sounded right. "Because you were the most exciting man I had ever met." Just what he needed, she thought, something to feed his ego. "Because something just seemed right for us. And because you were leaving the country."

That would have been the line he would have fed himself, Slade thought. "Is expediency a criterion in your lovers?"

If this was going to have a prayer of working—and of course it didn't, but that wouldn't be entirely her fault—then she had to be honest. "I don't have criteria for lovers."

"How about lovers, did you have those?" He saw the exasperated look entering her eyes. "Just learning a few facts about you, that's all. You can reciprocate with questions of your own at any time."

She looked at him skeptically. "And you'll give me an answer?"

"Yes." There was no hesitation.

Which aroused her doubts. "A truthful one?"

He grinned as he shook his head. "Where did you learn to be so suspicious?"

Oh, no, he wasn't going to use his charm to disarm her this time. "It's in my genes. I come from a long line of suspicious people."

Unable to resist, he feathered his hands along her face. She was wearing her hair down. He remembered that it had come undone that night, as well. He liked it that way, loose around her shoulders. "Were they all as gorgeous as you?"

She tried to pull away from his hands and found she couldn't quiet succeed. Or didn't want to. "You're changing the subject."

"No, I'm being charming." He buried his hands in her hair, tilting her face up to his. "People tell me I do that well." His breath whispered along her face, but he didn't kiss her. Not yet. "Charm them."

"I guess you do, at that," she breathed, anticipation dancing through her veins.

"Kiss me, Sheila," he coaxed. "Kiss me the way you did that night on the beach. Kiss me as if I were going away again."

She swallowed. If she were standing, her knees would have threatened to buckle. "Are you?"

Slowly, he moved his head from side to side. "Not anytime soon."

"But you will." And this time, she'd care, care desperately, she thought with a pang. She didn't want to care, didn't want to worry.

"On an assignment," he admitted. He was going to have to talk to Andy about reassigning him to the States again. "Not permanently." He tried to find a reason behind the look in her eyes. "Why, did someone leave you permanently, Sheila?"

"No." She had been the one who had done the leaving that one time. But there had been no other choice. "I never let anyone get close enough to leave." That much was true, she added silently.

Lucky for him, he thought. Playing with her hand, he raised it to his lips and slowly kissed each knuckle. "And why is that?"

It took her a minute to find her voice. He was good, she thought. Damn good. "My naturally suspicious nature, remember?"

"Everything." He tapped his temple as he released her hand. "I remember everything." His mouth hovered over hers, and she could taste each word. "It's part of my trade."

And then he kissed her, kissed her as if he wouldn't get another opportunity to do so again for a very long time. He kissed her like a bridegroom coming into his wedding chamber, like a lover who was reunited with a long-lost love.

He kissed her like a man who had suddenly realized that he had come into contact with the other half of his soul.

Her head was spinning so badly as she reached for him that she thought that she would fall off the bed, off the edge of the world. And she didn't care, as long as it was with him.

When he drew his mouth away, she clung to him, not wanting the kiss to end. But it had to. At very best, her body was a few weeks away from being able to let her do anything about the fire that thundered through her veins.

Sheila blinked, trying to focus. "Wow."

He laughed, but it was a kind, comforting sound. "I take that as a compliment. Now, go to sleep before I start calling around for a doctor who'll swear in writing that you're fit to render your wifely duties."

She could always forge the report herself, she mused. "What about my consent?"

"I just tasted it." He touched her lips with his thumb, not trusting himself to kiss her again, even lightly. "Right there. Good night, Doc." Kicking back the covers, he slid under them.

Sheila shook her head, not knowing what to make of him. "Good night, Garrett."

His back to her, Slade tried to make himself comfortable. "Pleasant dreams."

Frustrated ones, at any rate, she thought, looking at his back. With a sigh, she turned on her side, away from him.

She sincerely doubted she'd get any sleep tonight.

Chapter Seven

The night had gone surprisingly well. Sheila had been convinced that she wouldn't get a wink of sleep, not lying beside Slade. But self-preservation instincts had taken over. Sheila was asleep within minutes. Rebecca's plaintive demands for food had woken her up three times.

After the seven o'clock feeding, Sheila decided to remain up. Taking the baby with her, she went into her bedroom to change. The bed was empty.

"Wonder if he made a break for it," she murmured to Rebecca. Propping her daughter up in an infant seat she'd placed on the floor, Sheila quickly got dressed.

It still felt so odd to think of herself as married. Having a baby was an adjustment in itself, but she'd had nine months to become accustomed to that concept.

This was like finding herself in the middle of a hurricane moments after she'd looked up to see a clear blue sky darkening.

Sheila quickly brushed her hair and glanced in the mirror. It would have to do for now. She'd put her makeup on when she could focus.

Squatting before the seat, she opened the belts strapping Rebecca in. She wanted to hold her daughter against her, not have her encased in plastic.

"Well, let's see about getting some tea into your mother to get her going this morning."

Rebecca greeted her statement with wide eyes.

"Good, I like a receptive audience."

It was incredible how naturally Rebecca seemed to fit into the space formed by the crook of her arm, Sheila thought as she went down the stairs. She lightly pressed a kiss to the baby's neck, inhaling the sweet baby scent. Whatever else happened, she was going to be eternally grateful to Slade for the way she felt right at this moment.

Turning toward the kitchen, Sheila barely missed colliding with Slade. He was dressed in beige chinos that appeared to have been molded to his body and a dark brown shirt that accentuated his eyes even more. As if, with his dark, long lashes, he actually needed that.

Slade caught her by the shoulders, steadying her. His eyes touched hers. Sheila felt a shiver travel through her, more intimate than if he had actually made physical contact.

"Hi." Slade looked at Rebecca. The baby's expression was a disgruntled one, as if she'd missed her favorite program on TV. "And good morning to you, Short Stuff."

He'd shaved, Sheila noticed. The faint five o'clock shade was gone, and a light scent of cologne clung to his skin. She tried to place it and couldn't. "You're leaving?"

He nodded, checking his back pocket for his wallet. "Just for an hour or so. I've got some things to do down at the paper."

Without thinking, she brushed away a stray crumb from his shirt. Toast. Was that all he had for breakfast? God, there were so many things she didn't know about him, or about this situation in general. How did one go about being a wife, anyway?

When he raised a brow at her action, she dropped her hand, trying not to appear self-conscious. "I thought you were on vacation."

"I am. If I wasn't, I'd be catching a plane to somewhere."

That was something he was planning on discussing with Andy today. Getting off the foreign assignment chart. Jake Seavers had accompanied him overseas on several different occasions. He was still a little raw, but there was a lot of potential in him. He was probably ready and eager to go out on his own. Young, unattached and willing to take risks, he could be the new foreign correspondent. Slade was ready to surrender the mantle.

The baby began fussing. He laughed and kissed the light halo of dark hair.

"Hey, Short Stuff. Some fuss you put up last night. Great lungs." He looked up at Sheila. "Takes after my mother," Slade told her. "She was going to be an operatic singer until she met my father."

All she knew about his mother was her name. And that she apparently had raised Slade by herself. "The man who ran out on you."

The sympathy in Sheila's voice warmed him. It also made him uncomfortable. He shoved his hands into his back pockets. "Yeah."

Sheila looked around Slade's shoulder and saw the empty plate on the kitchen table. "I guess you've already had breakfast."

He grinned, glancing down at his shirt. She'd already deduced that much, he thought. "Just a quick bite. I don't usually care for breakfast."

Baby in one arm, she moved the plate from the table to the top of the dishwasher. "You see, that's another thing I don't know about you." Slade opened the door to the machine for her. Thinking better of it, he took the plate and placed it on the rack. "I don't know if you like big breakfasts or little breakfasts, or how you take your coffee—"

She was funny, he thought. And she cared. Boy, talk about falling into something good. It looked as if the luck that had faithfully dogged him all of his days was still intact for him. It had to be for him to have become entangled with a woman like Sheila.

"I like my breakfast small and my coffee thick and black." He tucked a lock of her hair behind her ear. An ear he wanted to nibble on. "And things like that are just minor matters—"

She freed the lock. "No, they're not," she contradicted him. "They're what make a marriage work. The tiny nuts and bolts."

"Nuts and bolts," he repeated with an amused frown. "We're not talking about a machine. Love is what makes a marriage work," he insisted. She'd yet to tell him that, he thought. That she loved him. But she would. "Love and understanding."

He bracketed her shoulders between his hands, peering at her face. She really did look unsettled, he thought, though he supposed he couldn't blame her. She hadn't slept much. The baby had summoned her three times by his count. Because of the intervals, he knew that each time was for a feeding. Once the baby was on a bottle at night, he could take some of the stress off Sheila and let her get some sleep.

"Is this a postpartum, normal thing you're having, or should I be worried?"

She paused, then let out a long, weary breath. That was exactly what she was having. A postpartum mood swing. She should have seen it coming.

"Yes, it's normal. And I'm not generally this emotional." She should apologize for being so contradictory, but she hoped that this would suffice.

Slade hugged her to him before releasing her. "I don't mind. See you in a little while. You too, sport." He touched a fingertip to the baby's nose. "Go easy on your mother. She's new at this. 'Morning, Ingrid." He nodded at the young woman as he passed her on his way out.

Ingrid, her long blond hair caught back in a ribbon, looked ready to take on the world. "Good morning, Mr. Pollack."

"Garrett," he corrected her, tossing the surname over his shoulder with the ease of a man who had no identity crisis to reckon with. He was secure in who he was.

More secure, he thought as he walked out of the house, than he had ever been before. This marriage business was agreeing with him, he mused. If he'd known that it could be like this, he wouldn't have avoided the situation for so long.

But then, it was only being married to Sheila that was making it right, he thought as he got into his car. Even rumpled and sleepy-eyed, she was more exciting than a centerfold in one of those men's magazines.

Looks like he was going to have to find a home for his own collection. He pressed the garage door opener and waited as the door slowly rose. The collection, one he'd inherited, unbeknownst to his mother, was just gathering dust in the storage unit, anyway. He'd kept it more out of nostalgia than anything else. His older cousin had passed it on to him, initiating him into the rites of manhood by conducting some very vivid anatomy lessons via visual aids for him when he was just thirteen.

Maybe Seavers could do the magazines justice. It was either that, Slade thought, starting up the car, or bringing the whole lot of them to a recycling area.

Seemed a shame, though. The magazines had been old when his cousin had given them to him. That made some of the issues more than twenty years old at the very least. Seavers it was. Though the magazines were tame by today's standards, Seavers would appreciate the collection. He was a nostalgia buff.

Whistling, Slade pulled out of the driveway.

Ingrid had immediately begun cleaning up the kitchen. Slade had left the loaf of bread and stick of butter out by the toaster. She returned each to its proper place.

She smiled at Sheila as she worked. "He is nice, your Mr. Garrett."

Sheila was about to correct Ingrid, saying that Slade wasn't "her" Mr. Garrett, but she stopped abruptly because he was. He was her Mr. Garrett, she realized. For better or for worse. She'd signed the license yesterday, surprised that he had managed to obtain one so fast. That made it official.

That same, uneasy, tightening feeling that she'd felt before when she took stock of what she'd done threatened to take hold of her again. Sheila banked it down.

"Yes, he is," she agreed. "Very nice. When he wants to be." She turned her attention to the baby. "So, princess, what'll Mom have for breakfast to help her face up to this new position of hers, hmm?" She opened the refrigerator.

"Oh, please, you have your hands full. Let me make you breakfast," Ingrid insisted, gently moving Sheila out of the way.

"I'm paying you to be a nanny, not a housekeeper," Sheila reminded her.

Ingrid remained undaunted. For such a sweet-looking little thing, she seemed very determined, Sheila noticed. "I can be both, Dr. Pollack. Now, what will you—?"

She stopped as the doorbell rang.

Slade, Sheila thought. He must have forgotten something. But why wasn't he using his key? She'd given him one last night just after dinner.

"Wait, I will get it," Ingrid offered, hurrying to the front of the house.

Sheila opened the refrigerator again. "There're too many people running around this house, Rebecca," she confided in a low tone. "I'm not used to this."

"Dr. Pollack?"

Sheila looked over her shoulder to find that Ingrid had returned. There was a huge, enigmatic smile on her face.

Now what? Sheila wondered. "Yes?"

In response, Ingrid took a step to the side. Needlessly, she announced, "Your parents."

Behind her stood Susan and Theodore Pollack. Together. Sheila's mouth dropped open. They were only together at functions. Did she now come under that heading?

She also couldn't ever remember seeing either of them dressed so casually. There were no family picnics to look back on, or trips to the beach or the mountains to remember. In a land noted for its resorts and vacation hot spots, her parents had only worked, not played.

But even in casual clothes, there was the air of refined class about them. Class, and something else. Something had changed, Sheila realized as she came forward. She could see it in her mother's eyes.

They almost looked like any other parents. Almost, but not quite.

Susan Pollack covered her mouth with her long, delicate fingers, and Sheila thought she saw what appeared to be tears shimmering in her mother's sapphire eyes.

"Oh, my God, Ted, it's true." Susan glanced at her husband to see if he was affected, as well. "She's had the baby."

Not waiting for a comment from the man she'd been married to for almost thirty-five years, Susan surrounded her only child, hugging both Sheila and the baby at the same time.

Those were tears, Sheila realized. Her mother was actually crying. She didn't remember her mother ever *crying*.

Susan pressed her lips together to suppress a sob. "Fine thing, having to find out that I'm a grandmother from an answering machine."

Sheila had called her parents as soon as she'd been brought in from recovery. A machine had picked up on the other end. She had expected nothing less.

"Hello, Mother."

Sheila lifted her face for her father's quick kiss and was surprised when he squeezed her shoulder, too. Were his eyes glistening, as well? Was it allergy season already? It had to be. Her parents didn't react emotionally to situations. They dealt logically with everything.

"You were away on a cruise," Sheila reminded her mother.

That in itself was unusual. Her parents never took time off from their practices, unless it was to attend a medical convention where, like as not, one of them was keynote speaker.

What was going on?

"You could have patched through a call to the ship," Susan admonished. "Celeste knew what cruise line we were on," she said, referring to the housekeeper. And then any reprimands faded away as she looked again at her granddaughter. "Oh, she's beautiful." Susan raised her eyes to her husband. "Isn't she beautiful, Ted?"

Settling comfortably into middle age the way he'd never managed to do with his youth, Dr. Theodore Pollack II smiled expansively. "Yes, she's beautiful. Not the way Sheila was, of course." He looked at his wife as if he was just now seeing her after all these years. "But then, Sheila had your eyes and mouth. Though this one has your name."

Susan smiled, and Sheila could have sworn she was blushing. "Rebecca Susan is a wonderful choice, dear," Susan said to her.

Sheila couldn't stop staring at her parents. It was like being zapped into the twilight zone. Or having one of her own fantasies suddenly take on a life of its own. The one she'd had as a child, where her parents behaved like a normal, loving couple instead of a reserved, professional one.

"Mother, Dad, is something wrong? You're behaving so... strangely." She couldn't put it any better than that.

Ted laughed, but it was Susan who spoke. "You mean we're not being stuffy?"

Sheila wouldn't have insulted either of them for the world, although that was the first word that came to mind. Stuffy. Reserved. Undemonstrative. "I mean, you're different. I expected a card with a savings bond, not a visit."

"The savings bond." The phrase suddenly triggered Susan's memory. She looked at her husband. "Did you remember to buy it?"

Sheila held up her hand before her father could answer. "That wasn't a hint, that was an observation." She stepped back to get a better look at both of them. "What's happened to you two?"

They exchanged looks, and then, to Sheila's everlasting surprise and pleasure, her father slipped his arm around her mother's shoulders. "I think that after thirty-five years of married life, we've finally found each other."

"The house was big, but not that big," Sheila pointed out. It had to be something more.

Susan settled comfortably against the crook of her husband's arm. "No, but our careers were. I don't think either one of us has to tell you that."

No, their careers always took precedence over everything. Her father's semiannual flights to Third World countries to perform operations on children who would otherwise have spent their lives impaired and crippled, her mother's weekly visits to the free clinic in the inner city, the long hours they spent at their individual practices, all this bit such a hole into the fabric of their lives together. But Sheila had adjusted to that, made her peace with it. This was just the way things were. Tigers had stripes, the sun rose in the east, and her parents were dedicated.

What had changed?

"So? What happened?"

Susan looked at her husband, deferring the explanation to him. It was too painful for her to repeat.

Ted paused before answering. It had been the very worst time in his life. Luckily, it had had a happy ending. But it might not have had. And no one knew that better than he.

"We thought your mother had breast cancer."

It was the first hint of it that she had heard. Sheila's eyes grew huge. "Mother!"

Susan held up her hand to stop the rush of words and questions she knew was coming.

"We didn't tell you, Sheila, because we didn't want you to be alarmed. It turned out to be benign. As, we realized, was our marriage." She looked at her husband, and there was no missing the love in her eyes.

"Both of us were suddenly faced with a very different picture of life than we were accustomed to," her father continued. "It was time for taking stock, time to look at what was really important."

"Each other—" Susan picked up the thread of the narrative "—and you." Her mother kissed her temple with more feeling than Sheila could ever remember. "Poor you. You were always shortchanged while I was rushing off to heal the sick and your father was flying off to Third World countries to perform his operations."

Sheila had always attempted to hold on to just the positive aspects of her childhood. "I was very proud of you," she told them honestly.

Susan combed her fingers through Sheila's hair. "And very lonely. I see that now. Charity begins at home, and you hardly got any." Her eyes seemed to caress her granddaughter. "Things are going to be different now that she's here." Susan grinned as she took the baby into her arms.

"Very different." Sheila couldn't remember ever seeing her mother grin, only smile absently. "We're going to spoil her rotten."

"Oh, God," Sheila feigned a groan. She looked at her father for help. "Dad?"

He laughed, enjoying this. Enjoying his life with the zeal of a man who had almost lost everything he held dear. "I'll keep her in line."

"Ha!" Susan scoffed at the promise. "You don't know your father once he gets going. We'll have to buy Rebecca Susan a condo just to house the stuffed animal collection alone."

Pleasure filled out every corner of Sheila's being. These were her parents, vying for the honor of spoiling her daughter. Incredible. "I think, for a while, I might like that."

Susan looked around the kitchen, as if she was expecting someone to pop out of the pantry. "So where is he, this husband of yours?" She turned to look at Sheila. "Or was that a glitch on the machine?"

Sheila shook her head. He'd probably get a kick out of being referred to that way. "No glitch. Slade's at work."

Ted nodded, a somber expression on his thin face. He pushed his glasses up the bridge of his nose. "Well, at least he's not a freeloader."

Amusement played on her lips. Her father had never expressed any concern about the men she went out with and their designs on her when she was living at home. "He's a journalist, Dad. Slade writes for the *Times*."

Susan waved away her husband's words. "That's just your father's sense of humor, dear. It's a little rusty. He hasn't used it in years. Give him time."

She smiled at her daughter. So much to make amends for. Where did she start, now that she'd been given this gift of life back into her hands?

Susan pressed her granddaughter to her breast, absorbing the comforting warmth. "Is he good enough for you, dear?"

The answer was immediate. Her mother never knew about Edward. There'd been no reason to tell her. At first, because they didn't really share confidences, and then because they didn't really share grief.

"Well, no, but the pope wasn't free so I had to settle for second best."

"The humor she gets from me," Susan told her husband firmly. Sheila was happy, she could see that. Susan's relief was immeasurable. It could have gone another way so easily. So many of her colleagues had children with messed-up lives.

She looked down at her granddaughter. "And this tiny dimple in her chin." She touched it lightly. "Is that his?"

Sheila nodded.

"Very nice," Susan said approvingly. She linked an arm through her daughter's, still holding her grandchild. "Come into the living room, Sheila. We're settling in for a nice, long visit. Walter's taking over my patients, and your father's partner is covering his. With you on maternity leave, none of us will be interrupted by that infernal beeping." There had been times, even at her most dedicated moments, that Susan Pollack would have loved to have thrown her beeper into the harbor. "We can have a nice, long conversation.

"Oh, by the way, did I tell you that the baby can call me Grandee?" Susan smiled triumphantly. She'd never cared for the term *grandmother*. "It has a nice ring to it, and it won't make me feel so old."

Ted laughed and shook his head as he followed the women in his life into the living room. "You'll never look old, Susan."

Susan murmured an appreciative sound. Inclining her head toward her daughter's, she confided, "He has lines he hasn't even begun to try out on me." She glanced over her shoulder at Ted. "I am truly looking forward to the second half of my life."

Sheila could readily believe that. "Where did you get a name like Grandee?"

"It's a mispronunciation of grandmother." One of the technicians at the hospital had mentioned it recently in passing. The woman's granddaughter had run the words together. "I rather like it."

Grandee. It had a royal sound to it that rather suited her mother, Sheila thought.

There was a navy blue Mercedes parked in the driveway. The model was at least ten years old, but the car was in mint condition. He wondered who it belonged to as he hit the garage door opener and drove his car inside. The license plate on the Mercedes read MD X 2. One of Sheila's friends from the hospital was obviously dropping by to see the baby.

He grinned to himself as he thought how normal that sounded. After the life-style he'd been forced to live in the last few months, normal and mundane looked pretty damn good to him.

Wanting to wash up first before he met any of Sheila's friends, Slade let himself into the house through the garage. The bathroom was just off to the side, but as he turned toward it, he saw Sheila out of the corner of his eye. She was in the kitchen, getting something from the bottom shelf in the pantry. She was wearing slacks and bending over, giving him a very tempting view of her bottom.

It was Sheila's bottom, no mistake about it. He'd know it anywhere, he grinned to himself. Ingrid was smaller than Sheila, and almost painfully thin.

Giving in to whimsy, Slade snuck up behind her and grabbed her by the waist. She squealed in surprise.

"Don't you know you're supposed to be resting?" He laughed as he spun her around. His mouth was an inch away from making contact with hers when he stopped short, stunned. "You're not Sheila."

The gasp turned into a shaky breath before Susan laughed out loud. This had to be Slade. "No, I'm not." She smiled warmly at her son-in-law. Sheila had good taste. "And it won't be the first time that I wish I was."

Realizing that he was still holding the woman, Slade released her. She looked like Sheila, and yet, she didn't. Slade took a step back.

"Who—?" He regrouped, studying the woman's face. The resemblance was unmistakable. "Sheila didn't tell me she had a sister."

Oh, yes, she was going to like this man. "And with good reason. She doesn't." Susan ran her hand through her hair, patting it into place. Vanity had never been her strong suit, but she wished she had a comb right now. "I'm her mother."

"Susan." Theodore entered the room, looking from the stranger in his daughter's kitchen to his wife. "What's going on here?"

Susan turned so that she could thread her hand through her husband's arm. Was that just the slightest tinge of jealousy she saw in his eyes? How wonderful, after all these years.

"I believe I came very close to finding out what it was that made Sheila get married so quickly."

Belatedly, Sheila entered the room, hurrying over to her parents. This wasn't exactly the way she had hoped to introduce them to Slade, amid commotion and confusion. Nothing, it seemed, was going according to plan these days.

Humor tugged at Ted's mouth as he witnessed the distress he saw in both Sheila and her new husband's eyes. "Sheila, I think your husband is hitting on my wife."

"Whoa." Slade held up his hands, forming a T. "Time out."

Slowly, he looked from one parent to the other. He had seen them, albeit from a distance, the night he had met Sheila at the fund-raiser. These definitely did not look like the same people. They looked far too approachable and friendly. The couple who had chaired the affair had been handsome, but brittle. He couldn't have pictured either one of them in jeans on a bet.

"You're Doctors Pollack?" Slade paused, realizing that he had to sound like a blithering idiot. "How do you address a husband and wife team, both of whom are doctors?"

"In this case, Mom and Dad." Ted took Slade's hand and shook it heartily. "You know, I always wanted a son."

Susan looked at her husband in surprise. After Sheila was born, they had both agreed that she would be an only child. "You never told me."

There were a great many things they hadn't shared. But they would now. "I thought it would be unfair to tell you how I felt. You hardly had time for Sheila. Two children would have been impossible for you." His eyes shifted to his daughter's face. There was so much he had missed. So much he could never recapture. "Not that I didn't shortchange you, too."

There was a time she would have welcomed this. Now, a mother herself, she understood how it could have happened. Sheila raised her hand to halt the apology.

"Stop. No more mea culpa, all right? We start with a fresh slade—slate," she corrected herself quickly, biting her lip as she glanced at Slade. He was laughing at her slip.

"Fresh slate it is," her father agreed gamely.

A smile played on Susan's lips as she looked at her new son-in-law. "I have a feeling Slade is fresh enough as it is." She slipped an arm each through both her daughter's and her son-in-law's arms. "So, why don't we all go back into the living room and get acquainted? I was just getting some cookies out of the pantry before you frisked me."

Ted raised a brow as he looked at Slade. "He frisked you?"

Susan laughed. "Not in the biblical sense, Ted. You can do that later."

Slade lowered his voice as he asked Sheila, "These are your parents?" These were the people she said never even slept in the same bed together? They seemed pretty playful to him.

"I'm not sure," she whispered back. "I think I'll have Celeste check to see if there are any empty human-size pods lying around their house. In the meantime, I intend to enjoy these people, whoever they are." She grinned at her parents, fully intending to do exactly as she said.

Remembering, she looked at Slade. "Did you get everything settled at the paper?"

They were still negotiating over his new position. He'd tell her about it when it was all over. "For now," he murmured.

Sheila wondered what he meant by that, but for the time being, she was dealing with enough mysteries just entertaining her parents. She'd ask Slade about his vague answer later.

Along with a lot of other questions she had for him.

Chapter Eight

Sheila turned up the baby monitor beside her bed. Rebecca, bless her, was sleeping peacefully. Ingrid had just returned from her late class on campus and had gone to bed.

The young woman had passed Sheila's parents in the driveway on their way home. They had remained all day. Sheila couldn't remember the last time she'd spent an entire day in the company of either of her parents, much less both.

If she was given to pinching herself, she would have, just to see if this was all just a dream, after all. The day had had that kind of quality to it.

She watched Slade as he went to close the blinds. His muscles rippled as he tugged at the stubborn cord. Accustomed to having to sleep in his clothes, he didn't even own a pair of pajamas. Shirtless, he wore only cutoffs to bed. Very frayed cutoffs that clung to him like another skin.

Sheila crossed to the window and opened it. It was getting much too warm in here.

Catching Slade's eye, she smiled. He had gone out of his way to entertain her parents today, fascinating them both with some of his stories about his experiences as a foreign correspondent. Her father had countered with stories of his own. They weren't nearly as harrowing, but just as deeply moving. They got along famously.

All in all, it had been a great evening.

"My parents like you." They had both said as much to her as they took their leave.

Slade turned to look at her. A shaft of moonlight ate away at her nightgown, framing her body like a luscious silhouette. It made him ache just to look at her. He blew out a breath slowly. He'd made it this far, he could wait out a few more weeks, he told himself.

Maybe.

Turning down his side of the bed, he grinned at her comment. "Why not? I'm a likable guy."

No inferiority complex here, she thought with a laugh. "Have we decided that yet?"

He moved to her side of the bed, folding over the comforter. "Yes. We had a vote."

She arched a brow. Was he including Ingrid in this? "We?"

He nodded. "Becky and I. She's nuts about me, you know," he confided smugly. "So it's unanimous. You can throw your vote in on our side if you want to look good," he offered magnanimously.

What was it about this man that made her want to laugh, to forget about her responsibilities and go running barefoot on the beach? Was it just her, or did he have this effect on every woman?

Probably. But he was hers.

Or so he said, a tiny voice whispered, but she shut it away. She didn't want anything spoiling this.

She struggled to maintain a straight face. "That's the second time you did that. I'm beginning to get the feeling that I'm being railroaded."

The face of innocence, Slade pulled an imaginary cord overhead and cried, "Toot-toot." Then, before she was able to say anything in response, Slade pulled her into his arms.

Sheila saw the kiss coming a mile away. And waited for it. Maybe even ran toward it, she wasn't sure. One minute she was laughing, the next, she was up on her toes, her head tilted back, her mouth eagerly slanting against his.

Instantly, her blood heated and her head might as well have been an apple bobbing in a tub full of water for all the coherent thoughts that were occupying it. It swam as the kiss deepened.

The taste of his mouth was every bit as potent as it had had been that night they met.

Maybe even more so, because now he no longer represented the mysterious, dangerous unknown that she had jumped into with both feet. Now she knew what was waiting for her.

Or thought she did.

Yet every time he kissed her, the effect was that much more intense, that much more bone melting. Lord, but she wanted to make love with him. Never mind that she was struggling to get her life back in order with this new set of ramifications. Never mind that she had grown up believing that marriages never worked, never delivered the promise that was made.

Her parents had just blown that premise all to hell. Now what was she to believe?

Her heart, she thought, wanting to believe that with every fiber of her being. Her heart.

She sighed when the kiss ended, sorry that his lips had left hers. Knowing that for the time being, it was for the best. Why play with matches when you weren't allowed to make a fire?

"Yup, definitely railroaded."

It was comfortable in his arms. And safe, she thought. Funny that she should feel that way. She'd never thought that she needed to feel safe from anything before. But he made her feel safe. She nodded toward the bed reluctantly. For the time being, they couldn't do anything in it but sleep.

"Time for bed." She got in on her side, pulling the covers up around her. "I can get in maybe three hours before Her Highness wants me again." If she was lucky, she added silently.

Slade slid in beside her, trying to get comfortable. He frowned as he laced his fingers beneath his head, cradling it. He glanced in her direction.

"There's definite sainthood involved here." Sheila raised a brow at him quizzically. "Lying here beside you and acting like a Boy Scout. That has *got* to qualify me for some sort of heavenly recognition for valor above and beyond the call of duty."

Sheila leaned over and brushed a kiss on his lips. "Sir Galahad," she corrected him. "Not a Boy Scout. Some of the Boy Scouts I knew when I was growing up would have never earned a merit badge, unless it was in intentional groping."

She'd told him that she didn't sleep around and he believed her. But how many men had there been in her life? Had there been one serious lover before him? He broke a cardinal rule and asked. "Did they intentionally grope with you a lot?"

Without fully realizing it, she curled her body up against his. "They tried."

Yes, he could definitely see any red-blooded boy trying. There was a portrait of her as a teenager hanging in the family room, part of a family collage. He would be willing to bet that she'd never had an unpretty day in her life.

"But—?" Slade coaxed.

She laughed to herself as she remembered Billy Rafferty and where his persistence had gotten him. He wailed that his lip was going to bleed for days.

"I was a tomboy." She doubled a fist. "I had no brother to protect me, so I did it on my own."

He liked her independence, he thought. It struck him as a very sexy quality. Slade covered her hand with his own, then turned it over and examined it. It was a delicate hand, one that could have belonged to a surgeon or a gifted musician. And right now, it held him in its palm.

"Looks lethal," he teased. He brought her hand up to his lips and pressed a kiss against her knuckles. "Remind me never to go up against you." His eyes held hers. "I'm a pacifist."

She doubted if she had ever been gullible enough to swallow that one.

"Like hell you are." Not if she was to believe any of the stories he'd told tonight. Not that he bragged in any manner. It was more what he didn't say at times than what he did. During his stint overseas, he didn't just stand back and record the news. At times, he was part of it. Like the time he helped smuggle a family marked for execution the next day over the border during the night. She knew that Slade would only be a pacifist if there was no more injustice in the world.

It made her proud of him.

"No, really," he said, humor tugging at his mouth.

Unconvinced, she settled against him with a contented sigh. "I bet you raised a lot of hell as a kid."

The sigh played along the skin on his arm, stirring a shiver he had to control. "My share," he admitted. Slade thought that over. Actually, he'd probably given his mother a lot of grief in his time. "Well, maybe more than my share."

She felt her eyes beginning to drift shut. "I guess it must have been hard on you." She struggled to stifle a yawn. "Growing up without a father."

There was something they had to clear up. "Well, as a matter of fact—"

The yawn escaped despite her best efforts. "It was for me." Slade looked down at her, bewildered. She could see his reaction in the mirrored vanity. "There were times I felt as if I was growing up without a father or a mother. They were always out there, helping others." Her voice was growing low as sleep beckoned her. "I was proud of that, but jealous, too. I thought that I had to break a leg or come down with some fascinating diseases just to get their attention." She laughed to herself as she thought of her parents the way they were tonight. "I can't believe the transformation."

He had seen it on a minor scale, between the benefit and now. His arm tightened around Sheila as he felt her head begin to nod against his shoulder. "What triggered it?"

"Coming face-to-face with their own mortality, I guess. Discovering that they didn't have forever the way they thought they did." The way, she supposed, everyone did until they were shown otherwise.

"Funny, I always thought I did." Given his beat, he couldn't think any other way. Fear tended to paralyze. Slade kissed the top of her head. "Now I just hope so."

She leaned her head back to look at him. "Does this come naturally to you, or do you practice?"

He laughed, and she could feel the sound rumbling in his chest. "Every morning, faithfully, in front of my mirror. Why?" He pretended to be surprised. "Doesn't it flow?"

It flowed all right. And was as smooth as silk. "A little too quickly at times."

"That's just because I want to get it out before I get confronted with your rapier wit." It was one of the things he liked best about her, her mind. Of course, her body wasn't exactly shabby, either.

At moments, it was still hard to believe that he had actually committed himself to another human being. He supposed it was going to take time to get used to. He'd give it fifty years before throwing in the towel. "I bet you were a knockout as a little girl."

She wondered if he noticed that the photographs of her in the family room were all taken after she passed the age of twelve. "You would have lost that bet. I was painfully ugly as a child. Broke mirrors wherever I went."

He found that difficult to believe. Both of her parents were very striking. And there were her own looks to back up his assessment. "And they didn't try to drown you?"

She gave him a playful rap in the arm. She hadn't done anything like that in years, she realized. Many, many years. "No, they ran away, like I said. Actually, I was probably the reason why they spent so much time doing charity work. To atone for bringing an ugly duckling into the world."

He closed his arms around her. "Well, you've sure made up for it now."

She knew better than to argue with a compliment. Sighing, she turned her head toward his on the pillow. "Slade?"

"Hmm?"

This felt right, too right. Disappointment had to be right around the corner. And yet, she fervently hoped not. "Do you think we're going to make it?"

There wasn't a hint of hesitation in his voice. "Absolutely."

She wished she had his confidence.

Seeing her parents suddenly in love after all these years had shaken the foundations of the world she had built up around herself. Because of them, she had just naturally assumed that careers and marriage could not possibly mesh successfully. Now, after all this time, her parents were proving her wrong.

Why didn't that make her feel more confident about her own marriage?

* * *

The question became less and less important as she ventured carefully into each day and discovered to her amazement and vast pleasure that married life seemed to suit her. Dedicated, used to keeping long and ungodly hours, Sheila had anticipated going a little stir-crazy during her medical leave. She had also assumed that she would have trouble fitting the baby and, most of all, Slade, into her life.

Set in her ways, she was accustomed to doing things her own way. As was he, she knew.

When the compromises began coming along, they surprised her. She quickly learned that compromises were his specialty.

"Then you're all right with this?" she asked, surprised he was taking her request into consideration, much less in stride. She had asked if he could see about getting himself a beat much closer to home. She had no way of knowing that he had already reached the decision himself and that Andy was amenable to it.

Slade was not above giving himself brownie points when the situation called for it. He thought it only fair that he be there for his wife and daughter. If agreeing with Sheila's request made him seem heroic and selfless in her eyes, so much the better. The bottom line still remained the same. He was still going to try his best to be home as much as possible.

"I'm okay with it," he assured her. "Sure, I'll miss it," he admitted truthfully, and he knew he would. There was something almost seductive about danger. But so was Sheila. "But I'm married now. Both of us have to make some changes in our lives to accommodate each other. Otherwise, why bother getting married?"

Sheila looked at him, utterly stunned by what he was saying. Did he really believe that?

"When you live by your wits and every twenty-four hours comes with its own visa, which side of the bed you sleep on isn't all that important," he told her. She looked at him blankly. "Translated," Slade kissed the tip of her nose, "don't sweat the small stuff."

She laughed. "Very eloquent."

He locked her in an embrace that perforce could go no further. Yet. "I save my best stuff for you."

He made her warm when he looked at her like that. Without admitting it to herself outright, she was counting the days until she was healed sufficiently enough to make love with him. Time was moving much too slowly in that department.

Tilting her head back, she kissed him. "I certainly hope so."

She tasted of strawberries and passion. The former was thanks to the jam she'd just had on her toast, the latter was something he was looking forward to.

He raised and lowered his brows, leering wickedly at her. "Get your doctor's approval and I'll show you," he promised.

The temptation to give her a preview was enormous, but he'd only be torturing both of them. With a sigh, he released her.

"I'll have to go in for a few hours to talk to Andy. I know I can talk him into switching my beat, but it might require a trade."

"A trade?" She didn't quite follow him. "What sort of a trade?"

He'd already made his bargain with Andy, so he knew the ramifications. "The sort that dreams are *not* made of. I still might have to go away for a few days, but at least it'll be stateside." His mouth quirked in a grin. "If anyone shoots at me this time, at least they'll be cursing in English."

"Shoots?" she repeated uneasily. The whole point of his remaining in the country was to avoid danger.

He liked the fact that she looked uneasy. And that she worried about him. "Just kidding. But I will most likely be gone for a few days."

She was just getting used to having him around. The three of them were beginning to bond, to form a unit. And she'd discovered that she liked not sleeping alone—when she could get some sleep.

"Oh?"

Slade cupped his hand around his ear. "Was that a little remorse I hear?"

Sheila pretended to frown. "Not remorse, exactly."

Yes it was, he thought, pleased. "But what, 'exactly'?"

If this thing was going to work, she had to be honest, she reminded herself. "Okay, I'll miss you." Sheila turned her face up to his. "There, will that satisfy you?"

"For now." Slade rested his hands comfortably on the swell of her hips. "We'll work on 'destitute without you' for the next assignment." He nipped her lips quickly, savoring the taste. "I like strawberry jam." He winked at her. "Walk me to the door, wife."

"Yes, master."

"Good, very good."

She shoved him on his way.

Sheila shook her head, grinning to herself as she closed the door behind him. It was actually working out. Of course, it was only a week into the marriage, but she was getting a very good feeling about this.

And it wasn't just because her parents had vaporized her concept of marriage. No, what gave her hope that things would work out for the best was Slade.

She really wanted this to work now. She liked waking up in the morning beside him. Liked feeling his eyes on her when she looked up unexpectedly. This tall, brooding man actually had a sense of humor about everything. Sometimes sardonic, sometimes whimsical, and always witty. He made her see that every light side had a dark side to it. And that the converse was true, as well.

It was best, he told her, to concentrate on the light side. There was no point in brooding about things. That had surprised her. She liked the fact that he maintained a positive attitude, even after he had seen what he had of life.

Best of all, she liked the way he held their daughter, as if Rebecca was something fragile and wonderful.

All of that pointed to a good future together.

Maybe, as Ingrid had predicted as she had stared into the wayward tea leaves on the bottom of her cup one morning, they were meant to be.

Ingrid, with her sky blue eyes and her four-plus scholastic average, had solemnly believed in what she saw. "Tea leaves do not lie, Doctor. They have no reason to. You and Mr. Garrett were meant to be."

Meant to be.

The phrase echoed in Sheila's head as she walked into the living room. She could let herself believe that if she tried.

Sinking into the armchair, Sheila closed her eyes for a moment, remembering how she had felt that night as they talked and made love until the sun came up.

That was when, she realized, she'd fallen in love with him. She was just too busy at the time to notice. Her mouth curved as she continued remembering.

The ringing phone chased away her daydream.

"I'll get it, Ingrid." She hoped that the sound hadn't woken Rebecca up. By her reckoning, the baby still had two hours to go to her next feeding. Sheila propped the receiver up against her ear and shoulder. "Hello, Pollack-Garrett residence."

There was silence on the other end for a moment, then a woman asked, "Is Slade there?"

"No, he just left for the newspaper office. Can I take a message? This is Slade's wife."

It was the first time she had ever said that, Sheila thought. Slade's wife. How could such a small word have such a large effect on her? It still felt strange on her tongue.

It sounded even stranger to her ear. "Slade's wife?" The woman on the other end sounded delighted.

Well, at least this wasn't an old flame trying to track him down, Sheila thought, wondering if that was a touch of jealousy she was experiencing.

"Yes. What can I—?" She got no further.

"How wonderful! This is his mother. Rebecca." The woman spoke in a breathless staccato. "I can't tell you how delighted I was to hear that someone had finally managed to tame Slade long enough to get him to say 'I do.'"

Sheila began to protest that if anything, the circumstances had been the other way around, but she never got the chance.

"He said you were a knockout."

This was his mother, all right. She even talked like Slade, Sheila thought. She had a feeling that she was going to like Rebecca. "He tends to exaggerate."

The laugh on the other end of the line was rich and lusty. Definitely Slade's mother. "I have a feeling that he didn't. He used the same glowing terms to describe the baby. I just can't wait to see you both."

An in-law. She had an in-law. A mother-in-law at that. Life was tobogganing right along, she thought. "Well, why don't you come over tonight?" It was just past nine. That would give her a solid nine hours to pull herself together to meet her mother-in-law.

Rebecca laughed, sounding pleased at the invitation. "It's not that simple, dear. We live in Phoenix."

"We?" Was she one of those people who talked in the plural, or was there a pet coming along for the visit, too?

"Yes, my husband and I."

"Husband." The word caught Sheila off guard, but she recovered quickly. "Oh, you mean Slade's stepfather." He hadn't told her his mother was married.

"Stepfather?" Rebecca echoed. "Oh, my, no. His father. If Slade has a stepfather, I certainly don't know anything about it." She laughed at the idea. "Heaven knows, Lawrence is certainly enough man for me. He's just like

Slade," she confided, "except that he's getting gray around the temples. Melted my heart the first time I saw him." She sighed nostalgically, then continued. "What I was calling about was to ask you if we could come for a visit next month. Lawrence has some time coming to him then. I forgot to make arrangements with Slade when I spoke with him right after the baby was born."

Sheila felt numb. "Next month will be fine," she heard herself saying. She was on automatic pilot.

It wouldn't be fine, she thought. It wouldn't be fine at all.

Somehow, she managed to get through the rest of the telephone call, but she had no idea what she had said. All she could think of was what Rebecca Garrett had said to her in the first few minutes of the call.

She was coming with Slade's father.

His *father*.

"Damn it, Slade, you lied to me," Sheila said aloud, anger throbbing in her voice. She felt as if she was tumbling off the top of a pyramid. "You probably lie about everything."

Drawn by the sound of Sheila's voice, Ingrid peered into the living room. "Did you say something, Doctor?"

Sheila stared at the telephone. That was what she got for believing, for being gullible. She took a breath and exhaled it slowly, steadying herself.

"Yes." Sheila rose to her feet. "We're not drinking tea anymore, Ingrid. Your tea leaves lie."

Sheila didn't bother explaining it any further as she walked out of the room, passing the bewildered young woman. She had some packing to do.

The few hours Slade had anticipated turned into more than half a day. The twenty-minute meeting in Andy's office mushroomed and grew until it encompassed the better part of the afternoon. He'd called home to tell Sheila that he would be late, but Ingrid said that Sheila wasn't taking any calls. He wondered if she was ill.

It made him antsy during the meeting.

The downpour that accompanied him home didn't help matters any.

By the time he walked into the house, Slade felt tired and edgy. The ride back from the office had been a bear. There'd been three accidents on the road, tying traffic up in a huge, insurmountable knot. He was relieved to be back home again.

"Honey, I'm home," he called out, shutting the door behind him.

He nearly tripped over the suitcases standing like ducks in a row beside the door. His suitcases, he realized when he looked closer.

Sheila walked in from the family room, Rebecca in her arms. She'd been waiting for him to return all afternoon, waiting to have it out with him. Now that he was here, she was so angry, she had no idea where to begin.

Slade gestured toward the suitcases. "Am I going somewhere?" he quipped. He didn't like the look in her eyes, but he'd ridden out storms before.

"Yes." Her voice was stony, her expression unapproachable. What the hell had happened while he was gone? he wondered.

"How did you know?" he asked casually, as if the sight of his belongings all packed up didn't throw him. He had to leave in the morning, but it was only a seven-day jaunt. There was entirely too much luggage here. "Although, I think you went a little overboard. I don't need every single thing I own for a one-week trip."

Oh, no, he wasn't going to use his charm on her again. It was just a smoke screen. "Yes, you do. And it's not for a week, it's forever."

Maybe this was just a mood swing. If it was, it ranked as the mother of them all. "Did I miss something? Is this a parallel universe? Is there some stunningly handsome guy somewhere walking into a warm embrace right now in my place?''

Her eyes narrowed. ''Can it, Garrett. You've used up your charm.''

''No, I have a six-month supply I haven't tapped into yet.'' She didn't smile. This was serious, he thought. Whatever happened, this wasn't going to go away with a few quips. ''What's the matter, Sheila? Did something happen?''

Yes, something happened. I opened up my eyes. ''I had a telephone call today.''

He had no idea where this was going or what to expect. ''And—?''

''It was your mother. She wanted to know if she could come for a visit next month.'' Sheila's eyes held Slade's as she waited for him to squirm. His expression was impassive. He was one cool customer under fire, she thought. ''With your father.''

Chapter Nine

Oh, boy, Slade thought. This was going to take some very fancy talking on his part. She was angry and he couldn't really blame her, although it was actually her fault that he'd lied in the first place.

Before he said anything in his defense, Slade crossed to the doorway and called for the nanny. "Ingrid, could you take the baby upstairs, please? Dr. Pollack and I have a few things to discuss." By the look on Sheila's face, he didn't think the discussion was going to be a quiet one, at least not to begin with.

The next minute, Ingrid hurried into the room, a textbook tucked under one arm. There was a pencil peeking out from between the pages, a makeshift bookmark. Studying for exams, Ingrid felt a little harried at the moment, but one glance at the couple had her swallowing any words of protest she might have offered.

"Of course," she said quickly.

"It's time for her nap," Sheila instructed. She did her best to keep the anger out of her voice, but it was difficult, standing in the same room with Slade.

How could he? How could *he?*

It was Edward all over again. There were no words to describe how she felt.

Sheila gently handed Rebecca over to the young woman and waited until Ingrid left the room and was presumably out of earshot.

Then she gave it to Slade with both barrels. "We have nothing to discuss," she corrected him heatedly, her voice thick with emotion. "We got married under false pretenses. You lied to me. Case closed." With that, she turned her back on him and began to walk out of the room. She wanted to get away from Slade before her emotions overwhelmed her completely.

Just like that? Without giving him a chance to explain? To try to reason with her? It didn't seem like something she would do. But then, maybe he'd misjudged her, after all.

Slade grabbed Sheila by the arm and turned her around to face him. "I lied to you because you wouldn't marry me any other way."

He had lied, lied about something inherently important. He'd used her own feelings against her. And he'd do it again. Just the way Edward had. Edward, the bright, young, promising resident who had conveniently neglected to tell her that he had a wife and baby waiting for him in another state. Almost eight years in her past, it still stung to remember. She'd sworn to herself then that she would never be hurt like that again. And here she was, doing it all over again.

"So what does that mean? That I'm married to a liar? To someone I'm going to have to doubt every time he opens his mouth?"

He stared at her. He knew she'd be upset, but this reaction seemed to be totally out of proportion. "Aren't you exaggerating just a little?"

He thought it was a joke, she thought. Didn't he realize how violated she felt? If she couldn't trust him, what was left?

Damn you, Slade. I loved you. Now you've ruined that for us.

She raised her chin, forcing tears back. "Oh, I don't know, am I? You lied about something very basic, to a woman in labor—"

"I lied to you *because* you were in labor." He had to make her understand. His own temper began to fray at the edges. "There wasn't time to convince you, remember?"

She shook her head, dismissing his excuse. How could she have been so stupid as to actually let herself be talked into this? Wasn't one lesson enough? But at least then she hadn't married the man. Then she'd had the opportunity to walk away.

"All I will remember is that you lied to me. I *hate* being lied to," she said fiercely. "It undermines the entire foundation of our relationship. Now if you tell me that the sun is rising, I'm going to have to look out the window."

Damn it, what was the matter with her? Sure he'd lied, but it wasn't as if he had a wife and five kids stashed away somewhere. Just a father. A pretty damn nice father at that.

"I think that's a pretty safe bet." Sarcasm outlined his words.

It only served to make her angrier. And feel more betrayed. "This isn't funny."

"No, it's not," he agreed, struggling with his temper. Losing it wasn't going to solve anything. "And it's not logical, either."

He was good with words, she had to remember that. They were his stock and trade. Not like Edward, who'd been clumsy once he'd been discovered. That had been via the telephone, as well. She'd picked up the phone while he'd been in the shower. It had been his wife on the other end, asking if he was going to be able to get any time off to come home at the end of the month. It had been a hell of a coda to their lovemaking.

"Maybe not to you," she said coldly. "Maybe because you deal with lies all the time." She wasn't making any sense. Sheila sighed, dragging a hand through her hair. It was her fault, she thought. Her fault for believing things would be different this time around. "Look, I was pretty shaky about entering into this marriage. I still am."

She raised her eyes to his. Damn it, she still cared. More the idiot she.

"And you've just thrown an entire pile of blocks on the 'con' side of the scale. I need some time to work this out for myself." *Time to harden my heart against you and move on.*

He couldn't believe what she was saying. "So you're throwing me out?"

Sheila pressed her lips together. She wanted to, would have felt better if she could, but right now, she wasn't up to physically doing anything. Her whole body felt like a lead weight. "No, I'm ushering you out," she corrected him.

Playing for time, Slade nodded toward the window. "Into the rain?"

She blinked, surprised. When had that begun? "It's raining?"

He laughed shortly. "With all the yelling you're doing, I can see how you could have missed the sound of thunder." Slade jerked a thumb toward the window. The sky was completely black, and the tree right in front of the house was dueling with the wind and the rain, its branches swatting away the onslaught. "Right now it's pouring outside."

Yes, it was. And pouring inside, as well, she thought. "Why aren't you wet?" she asked numbly.

What difference did that make? "I stuck close to the eaves coming in." Slade blew out a breath. He didn't want his marriage to disintegrate over something petty and insignificant. He tried again. "Look, maybe I did lie."

Her head snapped up. Fire melted her numbness.
"Maybe?" He really thought it was nothing, didn't he? And
when there would be other women, would that be nothing
for him, too? "Hearing you're a bastard will be news to
your mother." Her mouth curved, but there was no humor
in the smile. "Seems she and the father you never knew want
to come and see the baby."

Damn. He'd called his parents with the news the night
Rebecca had been born. He wasn't a model son, but he always tried to stay in touch for the major events. And this
had been a major event with a capital M. He hadn't thought
it would backfire on him, not until he'd had an opportunity to tell Sheila the truth about what he considered a white
lie at most.

He scrubbed his hand over his face. "Did you tell her
anything?"

Sheila looked at him, incensed. Did he think she was as
heartless as he was? "What, that she'd raised a pathologi-
cal liar? No, I didn't. I didn't want to upset her." Her eyes
narrowed accusingly. "Which is being more considerate of
her than you were of me."

He had no idea how to initiate damage control. He'd
never been in a relationship that really mattered to him before. None of them had ever progressed to the level where
feelings were exposed and raw, as hers apparently were.

"Sheila, I tried to tell you."

Oh, no, he wasn't going to compound one lie with another. "When?" she demanded. "When did you try to tell
me?"

He wished fervently now that he had managed to tell her.
God, how he wished he had. "The other night, after your
parents left—" he began.

Sheila shook her head. The expression on her face told
him that he'd struck out his only time at bat. "No, I would
have remembered hearing you stutter out an explanation."

"I didn't get the chance," he insisted, his temper flaring again. Damn it, what was wrong with her? He'd lied for the very best of reasons, because he didn't want to lose her or the baby. Didn't she realize that? "I started to tell you, but the timing wasn't right."

Her look cut him dead. "Yeah, right."

"I thought that maybe you'd take it hard." He frowned. "Apparently I didn't even come close to guessing how hard. I didn't say it because I wanted this to have a chance of working."

Stepping away from him, she threw up her hands in exasperation. "How, by grounding it in a lie?"

He crossed to her and tried to put his hands on her shoulders, to hold her, but she shrugged him off. Sheila held her hand up in front of her to stave off any other moves. She didn't want him touching her, didn't want him confusing her.

"No, I said I need a little time to work this through for myself."

He sighed. Maybe it would be better to give them both a cooling-off period. He glanced at the suitcases. "You want me to go tonight?"

"No." She felt tired, weary. "Like you said, it's raining and I won't throw you out into it. Tomorrow is soon enough."

For just a moment, he succeeded in cupping her cheek before she pulled away. "You're making too much of this, Doc."

Despite everything, she still felt desire sizzle just at his touch. When would she learn?

"Am I?" Her eyes challenged his. "You forget, I don't have that much material to work with yet. You're sexy, charming, and under pressure, you lie. How do I know that you don't do that constantly?" She already knew that he did. Once a liar...

This was serious, he thought. Very serious. And he had no way of fixing it.

Slade shook his head. "I don't have any answer for that, Sheila, except that you have my word that I don't."

"Your word," she repeated. Did he think she was a complete fool? "Your word." Her disbelief drew. "Garrett, I have no idea what your word is worth." She felt tears forming and squeezed them away. *Not now, not now.* "It's my own fault. I shouldn't have said yes."

"But you did." His voice was deathly still.

She banked down her unease. Edward had railed at her when she'd confronted him with his lie. And tried to hit her. Sheila's eyes were steely as she looked at Slade. "I can say no just as easily."

"But you won't."

She couldn't believe his gall. "Oh? And why won't I?"

Slade gave it everything he had. He felt as if he was fighting for his life. The battle was no less perilous than when he'd been running to escape enemy fire. "Because at bottom line, you're as fascinated with this attraction between us as I am." His eyes held hers, searching for confirmation. Reaching out to her soul. "At bottom line, you know it's right."

Damn him, he was looking into her heart. She bluffed her way out. "Your bottom line must be a lot more secure than mine, because I don't know any of that. I feel like I'm groping in the dark."

"You don't have to be." Wanting to shake her, he kicked one of his suitcases, instead. Sheila jumped as it fell over, hitting the tile. "Open your eyes, Sheila. Open your eyes."

Willing herself not to back away, not to give in to fear— or desire, she shouted at him. "They are open. And I'm not sure I like what I see."

Slade sighed, shoving his hands impotently into his pockets. This wasn't going to blow over tonight. Not by a long shot. "All right, where do you want me to sleep tonight?"

Sheila drew herself up. She'd won. But the victory felt incredibly hollow. "Anywhere but in my bed." With that, she turned on her heel. "If you're hungry, Ingrid made some stew. It's in the refrigerator."

He wasn't hungry, but he supposed he had to eat. He'd only had a burger all day. With a shake of his head, Slade headed toward the kitchen. "And the condemned man ate a hearty meal."

Sheila heard him and squared her shoulders as she continued walking up the stairs. She didn't cry until she reached her room and shut the door.

He was gone by the time she came downstairs the next morning. Slade had spent the night on the sofa. There was no bedding to indicate that—she doubted that he'd used any—but Sheila could detect just the lightest whiff of his cologne still clinging to the cushions.

Without thinking, she drew a deep breath and felt a instant reaction tingling over her body. She doubted that she would ever be able to smell that brand of cologne again without thinking of him.

Without wanting him.

"Like Pavlov's dog," she muttered under her breath. But that would have to change.

Sheila dragged a hand through her hair as she padded, barefoot, into the kitchen. She wasn't going to let it get to her. Wasn't going to let him get to her. She'd made a mistake. A major one, but it wasn't anything that couldn't be undone.

Except for the best part. Rebecca.

It was better this way, she told herself. Better that she find out now that he was a liar than later, when there was a lot more at stake.

Like there wasn't anything at stake now.

Sheila sank into a chair at the table, feeling as if she'd suddenly been deboned.

Did she really want to undo it? Did she really want a divorce?

Everything pointed to yes. Except for her heart. She just didn't know. For the first time in her life, things weren't clear in her mind. Even with Edward, the stinging realization that she had been used had been quick, sharp, as had the break. She never looked back, never took one of his phone calls.

But this time, she was torn. She honestly didn't know what she wanted to do.

"Good morning, Doctor." Ingrid breezed into the kitchen. Hair piled haphazardly on her head, dressed in shorts and a faded blue T-shirt, Ingrid looked as young as springtime. "You look as if you need some coffee," she diagnosed briskly. Ingrid poured her a cup. "Mr. Garrett just left." She placed the cup in front of Sheila on the table. "What shall I do with the suitcases?"

Cup raised to her lips, Sheila abruptly stopped and looked up at Ingrid. "Suitcases? I thought you said he left."

"He did." Ingrid placed her own breakfast plates into the dishwasher. "But he did not take all of them, only the small one. The others are still standing beside the door where they were last night."

He thinks he's coming back. Damn, that bastard, he thinks he has me wrapped up around his finger.

Never mind that she was undecided about the future. He wasn't supposed to feel so cocky after what he'd done. He wasn't supposed to think that he could just come waltzing back as if nothing was wrong.

Sheila set her cup down. "Leave them there," she told Ingrid. "He can pick them up when he gets back from wherever it is he's gone." That'd teach him to be so cavalier.

She realized with a pang that she didn't even know where he'd gone. He hadn't told her. She hadn't given him the opportunity to tell her.

How to mess up your life in one easy week, she thought sarcastically. She could give lessons.

Sheila could tell by Ingrid's expression that the young woman thought this was a little odd to say the least, but mercifully she was too well mannered to point something like this out. Sheila wasn't up to any explanations.

Ingrid merely nodded. "Of course, Doctor. I will tell my mother when she comes today."

Today was the woman's day to clean, Sheila thought. She'd completely forgotten. She usually wasn't home when Mrs. Swenson came to do housework. She didn't want to be here now. Eva Swenson liked to talk, and more than that, she liked to listen. She would be asking questions about the baby and Slade the moment she walked in.

She looked out the window. Last night's rain was a thing of the past. The sun was shining into the kitchen, bathing everything in a warm glow.

So why did she feel so cold?

She had to shake this feeling of bereavement, Sheila told herself.

"It is a beautiful day, is it not?" Ingrid was saying as she poured a cup of coffee for herself.

"Yes. Yes, it is," Sheila agreed with feeling. She rose to her feet. It *was* a beautiful day, and she was going to celebrate it by dressing Rebecca up and taking her to the office to show her off.

Just the way, she thought with a smile, so many other mothers had done when they brought their baby in for her to see.

"Ingrid, Rebecca and I are going out. If I don't get back in time, say hello to your mother for me."

"Do you want me to get Rebecca ready?" Ingrid offered. "I just love dressing her. It is like having a living doll to play with."

Sheila laughed softly. Ingrid was little more than a child herself, she mused, suddenly feeling aeons older. "No, this time I'll do it."

It would make her feel better, Sheila thought as she left the room.

Going in and showing off her daughter to her nurses and her partner made her feel wonderfully normal. But it didn't help alleviate the strange ache that was in her heart, or fill the emptiness inside.

"It's not because I miss him," she said to Rebecca as she drove back home. "He hasn't been gone long enough to miss."

But he was, she thought. She missed him terribly, and it was less than twenty-four hours since she'd seen him. Sheila supposed that made her a class A-1 idiot.

"Hello, what's this?" she murmured to herself as she turned the corner and drove down the street to her house. It was the last on the block.

There were three cars parked along the curb directly in front of and behind her driveway. She knew the people who occupied the condo next to hers were on vacation. At this time of day, her other neighbors were at work, or so she thought.

"Looks like someone's having a party in the middle of the day," she said to Rebecca as she pulled up into her driveway.

Sheila pulled up the hand brake and got out of the car. Coming around to the passenger side, she opened the rear door and picked up her baby.

This was her reality, she thought, holding Rebecca close. "Let's go home, Becky. It's been a very long morning." And the night, she thought, threatened to be even longer.

Sheila heard voices coming from inside the house as she put the key into the lock. Maybe Ingrid was having company, she thought. It didn't seem likely. Ingrid was the type to ask before taking liberties. But then, Sheila thought ruefully, she was second-guessing everyone incorrectly these days.

"Hi, Ingrid," Sheila called out as she turned to close the door. "We're back."

"Well, it's about time."

That definitely wasn't Ingrid. The voice sounded vaguely familiar. Dropping her purse on the floor beside the suitcases that were such a painful reminder of yesterday, Sheila turned around to see who the voice belonged to.

There were four women sitting in her living room. Four women and five babies divided between them. They sat surrounding the antique coffee table, which was covered with gaily wrapped gifts. Multicolored ribbons streamed down in profusion to the floor like saucy, tangled ringlets. All four women were her patients, and they had all recently delivered. The oldest baby there was only five months older than Rebecca.

For a second, Sheila was speechless. She crossed to the barely visible coffee table and looked at the collection of smiling face. "What are you all doing here?"

Marlene Bailey Travis, head of her own advertising firm, was accustomed to taking charge of situations. She was the first to answer.

"We wanted to see the newest addition to the baby-of-the-month club." She nodded at her sister, Nicole, and the other two women, women she had become fast friends with as they had all sat in Sheila's waiting room over the long months before their babies were born. During that time, Sheila had been more than just a doctor to them. She'd been a friend they could turn to with any questions, any time, night or day. It was time to show their appreciation. "Do you realize that between the five of us, we've covered the last five months in succession?"

Sheila, overwhelmed and pleased at this unexpected show of friendship, laughed. "The thought does occur to me." She looked from one woman to another. "So, how are you all doing?"

"Fine," Erin Lockwood was the first to declare. Shorter than the rest, she made up for it with her liveliness.

"Terrific." Nicole Lincoln beamed at her twins. Everything was terrific these days, now that she had the babies and Dennis in her life.

"Couldn't be better," Marlene attested.

"How about you?" Mallory asked. "Are you going to be able to make my wedding?" Mallory had sent her an invitation just yesterday. She stepped closer to Sheila, peering at her face. "You know, you do look a little peaked." She glanced back at her friends. "Anything any of us *experienced* mothers can help you with?"

"Oh, yeah." Erin laughed at Mallory. The latter had only been a mother for a month. "Like you really know what you're doing."

Mallory pretended to take affront and lifted her chin. "I'm learning every day." She looked at Marlene, the most sedate of the group, as well as the oldest. "And what I don't know, Marlene fills me in on."

"Hey, how about me?" Nicole protested. She held one baby, her son Ethan, in her arms, while the other, her daughter Erika, lay in an infant seat at her feet. "I've got two of them, that gives me twice as much experience."

"Or, put another way, twice as many opportunities to make a mistake," Mallory teased, a grin playing on her lips.

Marlene had learned how to walk the tightrope of delicate negotiations almost since the time she took her first step. Peacemaking was second nature to her. Setting her son into his infant seat, she cut through the good-natured teasing and stood beside Sheila.

The woman did look a little worn around the edges, she noted, and wondered if there was anything she could do to help. More than the others, she related to Sheila. The doctor was just as closemouthed about things that bothered her as she was.

"Anyway, the four of us all got together and thought that it would be nice to give you a baby shower—after the fact."

Not to be outdone by her sister, Nicole interjected, "Your nanny tells us that more congratulations are in order." Nicole saw the hurt look in Sheila's eyes before the latter could shut it away. Had she said something wrong? Feeling her way cautiously, she continued slowly. "She said you married Slade Garrett in one of those eleventh-hour situations." Afraid that she'd inadvertently said something wrong, her smile was a little forced as she added, "Nice work."

"Slade Garrett?" Erin echoed. This was news to her. She hated to be at the end of the line when it came to information about someone she knew. "Is that the same one who writes those articles for the *Times?* The one who always seems to be right in the middle of every war and conflict on the globe?"

Nicole studied Sheila's face. Was that what was the matter? Her new husband's career? "One and the same," Nicole assured Erin when Sheila didn't.

Marlene could only bite her tongue for so long. "Is anything wrong?"

Sheila shook her head. She wasn't about to be a wet blanket, not after everyone had gone to so much trouble.

"What could be wrong?" she asked brightly. "I have a beautiful baby and wonderful patients who bring presents and pay their bills on time. Life couldn't be better."

Marlene exchanged glances with Nicole. They'd both noticed that Sheila hadn't volunteered anything about her new husband, hadn't mentioned him in her litany of things she was grateful for. Maybe that was just an oversight. Getting accustomed to new routines and new men in their lives was something they all shared. All of them knew just how very tricky striking the right balance was.

Marlene placed her arm around Sheila's shoulders, silently communicating her support. One look into her eyes told Sheila that Marlene understood more than was being said.

"C'mon," Marlene urged. "We brought over a great cake. My housekeeper baked it this morning, and she said it's only good for a day. So we're all going to have to make the supreme sacrifice and finish it off before we leave."

Mallory was already on her way to the kitchen. "I think we can bear up to it, seeing as how it's an emergency and all."

Arms filled with babies, Erin and Nicole closed ranks around Sheila.

"Boy, we sure do make some cute babies," Erin commented easily as she looked at Rebecca, then back at her own son. "Must be something in the water."

Sheila thought of the beach the night she and Slade had made love. She struggled against the ache that threatened to overwhelm her.

"Must be," she agreed.

Chapter Ten

For the first time that he could remember, his mind hadn't been on his work.

The stint in Washington, D.C., couldn't be considered one of his roughest assignments. In comparison to the ones he was accustomed to, this was relatively easy. But even so, Slade had to constantly struggle in order to focus his mind on what was going on.

The situation at home invaded his thoughts with such regularity that Slade could have set his watch by it. Sheila's expression, a mixture of anger, disappointment and hurt, was one that he couldn't wipe out of his mind. He saw it waking and sleeping.

The more he thought about it, the more it seemed as if her outburst was a cover-up for something else. Something larger. His lie had triggered something within Sheila, something that was deep-seated. He intended to get to the bottom of it.

The thought that haunted him throughout his week's assignment was that he might lose her. Somehow he had to be able to find a way to make her tell him what was really wrong.

He desperately wanted to make this marriage work.

Maybe because he was so adamant about it, he'd screwed it up for himself, he thought. But he could fix that. He could fix anything as long as he had the chance.

His eyes felt really heavy as he drove the last leg of the journey home. It was a continuing battle just to keep them open. Slade could feel them trying to slip closed.

A paper cup semifilled with coffee, now cold, sloshed beside him on a cardboard tray. He'd taken the red-eye back from Washington, D.C. Altogether, that put him on his feet, or at least conscious, for close to thirty-six hours now. By this time, he was running on adrenaline, stale coffee and caffeine-laced cola drinks.

He'd covered terrorists letting loose some poisoned gas not too far from the Capitol itself from every conceivable angle that he could. His rhetoric brought out, in vivid colors, the fears of a nation that now saw themselves at the mercy of insane men with powerful weapons and causes.

Nothing that hadn't existed before, he knew, but it was something no one had ever said out loud until it actually happened. It brought home the fact that no one was safe, and, ultimately, everyone was vulnerable. Life was precious and had to be lived to the fullest. Now.

Covering the story, seeing the victims trying to put their lives together, those who still had lives to put together, helped Slade place his own problems into perspective. It convinced him that he was going to make his marriage work.

Slade exhaled loudly, drowning out the steady stream of nonstop chatter by the deejay on his radio. If he had to crawl and ask Sheila's forgiveness, he was secure enough in his own identity to handle that. It would be a start on the road to fixing whatever it was that was wrong.

If he knew nothing else, he knew he wanted this woman in his life. Permanently. Her, and the child they had created. The child who, within such a limited amount of days, had a stranglehold on his heart. The child who he intended to watch grow up.

And if any man came within five feet of her before she turned thirty, he'd kill him, Slade mused. With his bare hands.

His mouth curved. Especially if that man was a foot-loose foreign correspondent.

Slade's head jerked up. Damn, his eyes had almost closed. He blinked, hard, trying to keep awake. The headlights from the oncoming car in the other lane broke up like a high beam searchlight against his windshield, jarring him further.

He groped for the coffee and downed the remainder of the liquid. It tasted foul.

He was going to have to concentrate if he didn't want to wind up in the morgue with a tag tied to his toe, he upbraided himself.

The wise thing, he knew, would have been to pull over on the side of the road and get a few hours' rest. But anticipation made him anxious. He wanted to see Sheila tonight. Wanted to say he was sorry if he'd hurt her or had unwittingly dredged up bad memories with his lie. He wanted to tell her that he loved her.

Love wasn't something that developed gradually, not in his case. Love was something that came with the strength of an uppercut, hitting him square on the chin and demanding attention here and now.

He intended on giving it its proper due. He just had to convince Sheila to let him.

It felt like déjà vu.

It was raining again, just as it had the night before he left. This time, though, it was only drizzling. He let himself into the house quietly. The suitcases, the ones he'd left in his wake, were still there. Someone had moved them off to the side where they stood, like patient vultures awaiting their turn at the carcass.

The marriage wasn't dead yet, he vowed silently to himself. Taking a breath, Slade got a second wind.

He'd unpack the suitcases in the morning, he promised himself. Right now, he had something far more important than clothes to see to.

Making his way up the stairs, Slade saw that there was light spilling out into the hallway from the nursery. He smiled, glad he hadn't waited until morning to return home.

Good, Sheila was up. He wouldn't have to debate whether or not he should wake her.

One problem down, a hundred to go.

Very softly, Slade eased the door open.

Light from a small lamp threaded through the room, casting it into a mournful dimness. Sheila was pacing the floor with Rebecca, her face a mask of concern. The mewling noises he heard coming from his daughter sounded almost pitiful.

The cries of other children, children racked with illness and hunger, rang in his ears.

Something was wrong. He would feel the tension in the air. "Sheila?"

She turned toward him, startled. Worry had cocooned itself so tightly around her that she hadn't heard Slade come in. Hadn't heard anything but her baby's cries.

For a second, she thought she was imagining him. In the last week, she'd thought about him returning a great deal, vacillating as to what she would do and say, playing the scenario a dozen different ways. But now, something far more grave had taken precedence in her life.

The scent of his cologne, mingling with the smell of rain, almost made her cry. For the very first time in her life, she desperately wanted someone to lean on. And he was here.

"Oh, Slade, she's sick."

If he hadn't guessed, the look on her face would have told him before she uttered a word. He crossed to Sheila quickly, looking down into Rebecca's face. Even in the sparse light from her lamp, he could see that the baby's eyes had that ill cast to them.

The wails were weak and wrenched his heart.

"What's the matter with her?" Sheila was a doctor. Why wasn't she doing something instead of just pacing the floor?

The cold realization that perhaps there wasn't anything to do began to skim along the perimeter of his mind, but he refused to admit it in.

Sheila pressed her lips together, rocking her body, trying to lull Rebecca to sleep. It felt as if every coherent thought had fled her mind.

"She won't keep anything down. She's been throwing up and crying since early this afternoon." There was a catch in her throat and she struggled to talk past it. "I don't want to sound like a panicky new mother—"

This had to be hard on her, Slade thought. Hard for her to meld professional feelings with personal ones. He'd learned that lesson himself a long time ago, on his very first foreign assignment. The pain and suffering of children could never be forgotten.

"But you are a new mother," he insisted, "and sick babies are something to panic about."

He'd seen too many in his time, too many babies with eyes that had the same glazed cast as Rebecca's. Babies who died because there was no doctor to care for them.

Sheila knew she was behaving badly. She was a doctor, for heaven's sake. There was no reason to feel helpless like this. And yet, the longer she walked the floor with her child, the less secure she felt.

"I'm taking her to the hospital," Sheila decided suddenly. Originally hoping that things would get better by morning, she no longer wanted to wait another minute.

It was what he was going to suggest. "Let's go, I'll drive." Walking out into the hall, he wondered how Ingrid was managing to sleep through the commotion. "Where's Ingrid?"

"At her mother's house. Sick." Slade turned to look at her. "She has the flu." The young woman had come home from college on Tuesday, complaining of aches and pains. By Wednesday, she was throwing up. Her mother had come to take her to stay at her house. "There's something making the rounds, I heard." Her voice trailed off.

Sheila didn't realize how much she had wanted him to return home until very this moment. She didn't want to face this first crisis on her own.

Grabbing a blanket, she wrapped it around Rebecca. She hadn't bothered undressing for bed, even though it was past eleven. She'd been with Rebecca, walking the floor, trying to get her to go to sleep, for the better part of the evening.

Slade opened the front door for her. "I'm surprised you haven't taken her already."

She followed him to his car, parked in front of the garage. Sheila hunched her shoulders against the light mist, pressing the baby to her breast. Slade opened the rear passenger door for her and she slid inside. His suitcase was on the seat next to her. God, she was grateful that he'd returned.

Slade pulled the seat belt out, buckling Sheila in as she held the baby in her arms.

"I kept hoping that it would pass. It's only been a few hours," she confessed as he got behind the wheel. "But she hasn't been eating at all. She cries when I try to feed her." Sheila stifled a sob. "And she has such a healthy appetite."

"Takes after her old man," Slade quipped as he started up the car. He pulled out quickly. If a policeman stopped him, he could use the escort, he reasoned. Slade glanced at Sheila in the rearview mirror as headlights sliced through the car, illuminating her face. "Don't worry, it'll be all right."

He was reassuring her, she thought, a sad smile playing on her lips. "I should be the one saying that to you."

"Go ahead," he coaxed. "I wouldn't mind hearing it myself." He smiled, but he was serious.

Slade didn't want to share the fear that was ricocheting through him, a fear brought on by the memory of looking into the faces of children without hope. Children who had had their childhood torn from them by men bent on war.

Children who had died before they had a chance to live.

Sheila licked her lips. They felt so dry. "When I brought Rebecca into the office the day you left, Lisa mentioned that there was a strain of flu going around."

She was sure that somehow, she was responsible for exposing Rebecca to it. Slade could tell by the agony reflected in her eyes.

"It was my fault," she murmured to herself. "I shouldn't have taken her in."

"Why? Was there someone there who was sick?"

She shook her head. "No, but—"

"Then don't beat yourself up for it," he advised, his voice mild, even, as if he were talking a jumper from a ninth-story ledge. "Maybe she caught it from Ingrid, or even when she was still in the hospital." There were a lot of possibilities. "You can't put her in a plastic bubble, Sheila."

She knew that, but it still didn't help dissolve her guilt, or make her feel less helpless. "I know." Sheila's voice was low, filled with the tears of the helpless. "She looks so tiny."

That she did. But he wasn't going to dwell on anything that might happen. Life was too full of negatives. The only way he had ever managed to make his way was to concentrate on the positive.

"And before you know it," he told her, " she's going to be asking for keys to the car."

Sheila sniffed. If Slade could manage to keep a positive outlook, so could she. It was just that something so grave had never come so close to her before.

Her eyes met his in the rearview mirror. "I thought you were buying her a Corvette."

"I am." Stepping down on the accelerator, he flew through a light that had turned red just as his tires touched the white line. "But she'll want to drive before I have a chance to buy it for her. You know how women are," he said, tossing the words over his shoulder for her benefit.

The tires of his car squealed in protest, reminding him that he needed air in them, as he pulled up almost directly in front of the emergency room entrance.

The sleepy feeling that had been tightening its grasp around him was completely gone. Adrenaline was pumping through him, hard and fast, just the way it had when he'd been covering stories overseas.

Except that this time, the stakes were far more personal.

He was at Sheila's side before she had had a chance to even open the door. He took Rebecca into his arms as Sheila got out. The infant continued whimpering.

Damn it, this wasn't supposed to be happening. She was too young, too tiny, to fight off anything on her own. Sheila looked up at Slade, fear nibbling away at her nerves. "She sounds weaker."

"Four hours of crying can take a lot out of you," he quipped, only because he wanted to keep Sheila's spirits up. They hurried through the electronic doors.

Sheila's eyes never left her daughter's face. "So can not eating."

Just within the doors was a large, glass-partitioned waiting area. She'd never been through this side of the hospital doors before, Sheila thought as the warmth of bodies housed in close proximity enveloped her. She felt vulnerable and just as frightened as so many of the people who walked through here.

More, because she knew what was happening. And what could happen as a result. Rebecca was dehydrating. At her slight weight, it wouldn't take much for the situation to become critical.

The woman at the registration desk barely looked up, sensing their presence. "Have a seat, please," she instructed. "We're a little full up."

For the first time in her life, Sheila pulled rank. Maybe it wasn't right, but she didn't care about right. She cared about her daughter's life.

"I'm Dr. Sheila Pollack." The woman behind the desk looked up immediately. Sheila didn't recognize her. "I'm on staff at this hospital. Is either Dr. Williams or Dr. Mattox on call, please?" Her throat felt as if it was closing over. "I have a very sick infant here. She's my daughter."

She knew she should have thought to call one of the pediatricians first, but she couldn't seem to think coherently. It was as if everything in her head had been tossed up in the air in a bizarre imitation of fifty-two pickup.

As soon as Sheila mentioned the doctors by name, the woman quickly worked her way down the roster of physicians on duty that hung behind her. Neither doctor's name appeared on the board.

She reached for the telephone, dialing as she spoke. "I don't know, but I can find out." The woman saw an intern emerging through the double doors behind her. "Simon," she called to the young man. "Take Dr. Pollack and her baby in back, please."

Slade and Sheila followed behind the intern. "All kids get sick," Slade told her.

Sheila couldn't help wondering if he was saying the words to comfort her or himself. In either case, it only seemed to be succeeding marginally.

"It's just a natural process," Slade continued as the intern led them to one of the free beds.

Rebecca's fever was climbing. He could feel heat radiating from her tiny body. Slade couldn't remember when he had ever felt so lost and out of his element.

The intern looked at the bed ruefully, and then at the baby in Slade's arms. "I think you'd better hold her until we can get a crib down here." There were bars on the side of the bed that could be raised, but they didn't go up all the way. The baby could easily tumble out. "I'll see what I can do," he promised. "Be back in a few minutes." He disappeared behind the curtain before either of them could say anything.

Slade gently slid the palm of his hand along Rebecca's head, just barely coming in contact with her hair. He didn't want to disturb her. Worn-out, Rebecca had temporarily fallen asleep.

"She'd probably going to have to spend the night," Slade murmured to Sheila.

He didn't like thinking of Rebecca being here, with so many other sick people. This was his little girl. No matter what he said to Sheila, he felt she shouldn't have to be dealing with anything like this. But Rebecca needed nutrition to survive, and if she wasn't holding it down, she was going to have to take it intravenously.

"I know." She looked up at Slade. Gratitude for his support was in her eyes. She laid her hand on his arm. "So am I."

Slade placed his hand over hers. They still had a lot to iron out, a lot to discuss. But now wasn't the time. Now was only for Rebecca.

"So are we," he corrected her.

She swallowed and nodded. "Thank you."

"There's nothing to thank me for. She's my daughter, too."

The intern returned a few minutes later without the crib. He looked hopeful as he peered in behind the curtain. "Good news, Dr. Pollack. We haven't located a crib yet, and I'm afraid that Dr. Mattox is out of town—"

"And the good news would be?" Slade pressed impatiently.

"They've called Dr. Williams and he's on his way in right now."

Ben Williams. He was a good man, Sheila thought. He'd been a pediatrician for more than twenty years. He was Rebecca's doctor. Logically, Sheila knew that her baby would be in good hands.

But there was still that awful, shaky feeling inside, the one that wouldn't release her. Sheila nodded her thanks to the intern and he disappeared again.

Alone within the small confines of the curtained area, Sheila raised her eyes to Slade. To her husband. Everything else was forgotten.

"Oh, God, Slade," she whispered, afraid to speak any louder, afraid her voice would break, "if anything happens to her—"

"It won't." His eyes held her. "You have to believe that."

Sheila blew out a breath as she nodded. She believed. There was nothing else she could do.

"You know," she began slowly, needing to clear the air. "I thought that maybe you weren't going to come back."

"I had to. You had the rest of my things." He looked at her, his voice growing serious. "And my heart."

"Slade, about the argument—"

He had wanted to get it out in the open. Now, it didn't really matter. "Forget it. It's in the past."

"No, I can't forget it," she insisted. Her voice was low, but there was no missing the emotion in it. "I have to tell you."

"Tell me what?"

"There was someone else. Before you," she added. She hated remembering, but she owed him this. "It happened while I was a resident back east. He was the chief resident at the hospital where I was doing my work—" She paused, her eyes on her baby. Her sweet, precious baby.

This was harder for her than he thought. She was going through enough as it was. "You don't have to tell me now."

"Yes, I do. I want you to understand." She stared at the white curtain, seeing the past. "I fell in love with him. Trusted him. And he lied to me. Lied to me about his wife and daughter. Or actually," she amended, "he just forgot to mention them to anyone. His wife called one day while I was in his apartment, asking when he was coming home." She looked at Slade. "I answered the phone."

Just as she had when his mother called, he thought. The pieces all fell together. "So when you found out that I lied to you about my father—"

"I thought it was Edward all over again." But Slade wasn't Edward. They were a world apart. She knew that now. "I'm sorry. I overreacted."

"Under the circumstances, that's understandable." He looked at her. "Am I forgiven?"

She almost laughed at his expression. "You are if I am."

He smiled. "Done." He looked at his daughter. "She's going to be fine, Sheila. I promise. And I don't break promises."

Sheila merely nodded.

It was another thirty minutes before they saw Dr. Williams. Sheila thought she was going to crawl out of her skin, waiting. The doctor arrived, dressed in a tuxedo and looking none too happy about being called away from the closing-night party for the cast and backers of the play he'd been attending. The party was being held at a posh hotel across the street from the Performing Arts Center.

The blustery expression on his face softened considerably when he saw that it was Sheila who had summoned him.

"Hey, I just saw this little lady last week. She was fine then." His hamlike hand seemed to encompass Rebecca's entire head as he laid a palm to her forehead. He frowned. "How long has she been like this?"

Sheila quickly recited the symptoms and when she had noted their occurrence as the pediatrician checked Rebecca out. Awakened, the baby began crying again. Slade thought he had never heard such a mournful sound.

"I think she has the flu that's going around," Sheila concluded. "Besides her temperature, she hasn't held down anything for the last twelve hours."

"It's the flu, all right." Taking off his stethoscope, he draped it over his neck. It looked out of place with his tuxedo. "We're going to have to keep her until she licks this, Sheila."

Sheila nodded. "How long will that be?"

He shrugged. "A day, several. Maybe a week. There's not much we can do at this stage except lower her temperature and feed her fluids. Good thing you brought her in when you did."

Dr. Williams's sympathetic look took them both in. "Don't worry, Sheila, your daughter'll be fine. I'll stay until they have her in a room."

"I appreciate that."

Dr. Williams called the intern over and gave him instructions for Rebecca's admission.

"Did we get you at a bad time?" Slade nodded at Williams's tuxedo.

"What? Oh." He looked down at his clothes. "No, you saved me from a banquet and gaining an extra five pounds I don't need."

Sheila saw the quizzical look in the doctor's eyes as he looked at Slade. In her anxiety, she'd completely forgotten to introduce the two men. "Ben, this is my husband, Slade Garrett."

The doctor took Slade's hand in his, shaking it heartily. The grin folded into the craggy wrinkles around his mouth and eyes.

"Oh, yes, the delivery room nuptials." He looked at Sheila. "That's going to make the rounds for a long time, Sheila."

"And here I was hoping to be remembered for my expertise," she murmured.

Dr. Williams finished writing his instructions on Rebecca's chart. "This way is far more colorful," he assured her. He flipped the chart closed, then hung it off the side of the bed where the orderly would find it when he took care of the transfer. "She'll be on the pediatric floor." He looked from one to the other. "There's nothing more you can do tonight. Why don't the two of you go home and I'll have the nurse call you if there's any change?"

She wasn't going to be ushered out. "I can't sleep, Ben. I'll just pull up a chair beside the crib."

Dr. Williams looked to Slade for reinforcement. "Can't you talk any sense into your wife?"

Slade placed a hand on Sheila's shoulder. Neither one of them was going anywhere. "No, I was going to ask her where I could find another chair."

Dr. Williams sighed. It was pointless to argue. "All right, you might as well bring her upstairs. We'll see about getting her a crib—and some chairs—now." He called over an orderly to strip the bed even though Rebecca hadn't made use of it.

He led the way out of the emergency room to the back elevators. "So," he began conversationally, addressing Slade, "rumor has it that you're a foreign correspondent."

"I am." *Or was,* he amended.

"What do you think of the situation in . . . ?" The doctor's voice droned on.

Slade tried to keep his mind on the conversation and not the shadow hovering over the infant in his arms.

Chapter Eleven

Dr. Williams had remained longer than he promised. He'd waited with Sheila and Slade until the preliminary test results were in to confirm his diagnosis. His initial diagnosis had been right. Rebecca had fallen victim to the latest strain of flu making the rounds. Her dehydration level hadn't become low enough to be critical, but they had needed to bring her in.

"It looks a lot worse than it is," Dr. Williams assured them, directing his words to both. Sheila might be a professional, but he knew it was different when it was her child lying in a hospital bed. He had three children and seven grandchildren of his own and he knew how frightening the feeling could be.

"I hope so, because it looks pretty damn scary." Slade leaned in over the metal bars of the crib. His daughter, her tiny arms immobilized to keep her from pulling out the tubing, was tethered to two different intravenous lines.

It was a sight to remind him just how fragile life really was.

"We're feeding her," Williams said. The explanation was needless, but somehow, still reassuring to hear. "This will keep her from dehydrating until she can retain liquids on her own."

Sheila nodded, knowing that everything that could be done, was being done. It still didn't help quell the uneasy feeling. She felt tears gathering in her eyes.

"She looks so helpless, so tiny." What if Rebecca didn't have the strength to fight the virus off? What if—? She couldn't complete the thought, not even in her own mind.

"Are you sure you want to stay here?" the doctor asked gently. "There's really nothing you can do."

He didn't have to say that to make her realize her own helplessness. She already knew.

"I can watch her," Sheila replied thickly. With the tip of her finger, she stroked her daughter's hand. "I can let her know that someone is here."

Dr. Williams nodded. He understood the need. "I'll be by in the morning to check on her."

Slade glanced up to see the man leave. "We'll be here."

Sheila and Slade stood side by side at the crib, looking down at the life they had created together. A life tethered to this world, it seemed, purely by IVs.

"I've never felt so powerless in my whole life," Slade whispered to Sheila, his eyes on the baby.

Impotence ate away at him. He couldn't help Rebecca, couldn't help Sheila bear up to this. He knew what she was thinking without asking. The same thought that was occurring to him. He'd seen too many babies die to take anything for granted. And Rebecca was burning up.

The emotion in his voice moved her. For the first time that evening, Sheila really looked at him. Exhaustion was etched deeply into his face. She reached for Slade's hand.

"Why don't you go home?" she coaxed. "You look dead on your feet."

"I'm okay." A ghost of a smile played on his lips. "That's why they call it the red-eye. Because of what you look like after the flight." He dragged a hand through his hair.

Some of her concern shifted. She hadn't stopped to think of how all this was affecting him. "When did you sleep last?"

He laughed softly. For a moment, he couldn't remember. "In another lifetime, I think."

Sheila shook her head. He needed rest. "Go home, Slade. I can stay here."

She wasn't getting rid of him that easily. This was his child as well as hers. She didn't have a monopoly on love, or concern.

"I know you can. So can I." Slade glanced at the coffee-colored vinyl chair the orderly had brought in. "I've slept on worse."

Sheila didn't doubt it for a minute. Not after some of the stories he'd shared with her. Though she was worried about him, as well, she couldn't deny that she was glad for his company. Glad to have someone to face this with. "Thanks."

She meant that, he thought. As if it was a favor he was doing. As if the fate of their baby wasn't as supremely important to him as it was to her. He sighed. She'd learn. He had a lifetime to teach her, and she'd learn.

Slade threaded his arm around her and drew Sheila a little closer. He kissed the top of her head. It was a purely affectionate gesture. Not one steeped in passion or desire, just affection.

It touched her more than she could say.

"Don't mention it," he murmured into her hair. "She's half mine, you know."

Sheila nodded, swallowing a lump that had suddenly materialized. She buried her face in his chest. "Which half do you want?"

"The top half. Until she learns to talk back." Holding Sheila even closer, he looked down at the baby in the crib. Humor left without a trace. "Seems incredible that something so small could have such a half nelson hold on your life so quickly."

Her soft laugh wafted along his shirt. He could feel it warming the center of his chest. Sheila turned her head to look at the baby. "I was just thinking the same thing."

With a sigh, Sheila stepped away and looked around the room. It was intended to accommodate three beds. One of them had been moved out to another room to make space for Rebecca's crib. The other two beds were empty. That gave them privacy.

She wanted to yell, to throw things, to rail at this invisible villain that caused her daughter's pain. She struggled to get her emotions under control.

Bone tired, Slade felt too restless to lie down. He recognized the feeling and knew it was useless to try to get any sleep yet. He had to wait until this steely tension relaxed its hold on him.

He felt his pocket for change. "Where's the nearest vending machine in this place?"

It took her a second to remember. She knew the hospital like the back of her hand, and yet she'd drawn a blank when he asked. "In the basement by the cafeteria." He began to walk toward the door. "But the nurses keep a stocked refrigerator on each floor just behind the nurses' station. What do you want?"

He looked at her. *To take my little girl and my wife home.*

"The usual. Coffee, black and thick." The way he figured it, he was up for the duration. He might as well resign himself to it.

There was always a pot of coffee going. She nodded. "They can accommodate you. Just tell them you're my husband."

A smile curved his mouth. It was the first time Sheila had called him that directly. He wondered if she realized that. They'd had their first major argument and survived that, he thought. The rest would be easy. As long as Rebecca was all right.

"Will do," he answered. "Does that entitle me to a sandwich, too?"

The hour was late. Sometimes the supply dwindled. And the cafeteria kitchen had been closed for hours. "If they have one. You're hungry?"

No, he wasn't. There was a hole where his stomach should have been. "I was thinking of you. When did you eat last?"

Her eyes met his. "In another lifetime," she echoed his phrase.

He'd guessed right. She wasn't looking too well herself. "That's what I thought. You need to keep your strength up." He saw her opening her mouth in protest. He expected nothing less. "You don't want to come down with this thing, too, do you?"

No, but it was a futile debate from where she stood. "I don't think I can keep anything down."

Slade crossed back to her. He touched her forehead with the back of his hand. It was cool, but that might not mean anything.

"*Are* you coming down with the flu?"

She liked the look of concern in his eyes more than she thought she would. He made her feel cared for. "No, just a stomach tied up in knots, that's all."

That he could understand. But she still needed to eat. "Physician, heal thyself."

She was tired. She didn't think she'd ever been so tired before in her life. Not during those endless sessions on duty when she was a resident. Not even when she'd given birth. It felt as if she was literally turned inside out.

Under the circumstances, her temper was fairly volatile. She looked at him sharply. "What's that supposed to mean?"

He wasn't going to get into a discussion about it now. His nerves were too close to the edge for him to maintain control. Slade didn't want to end up shouting at her over nothing.

"It means that you have to take care of yourself. For Becky's sake. And your own." His eyes met hers. *And mine,* he added silently.

She turned to look at him. She'd treated him pretty shabbily that last night. She wouldn't blame him if he wanted to walk out. After all, she hadn't given him an explanation then why his lie had affected her the way it did. "Do you enter into the equation?"

What made her think she could get rid of him that easily? "I'd like to. My suitcases are still standing by the door, although I noticed they've been moved over more to the side."

That had been Ingrid's doing. And she had been tempted several times during those seven days to unpack them again. "I wanted you to use them. And then when I didn't, I was too busy with Rebecca to unpack them for you again."

He knew why she had gotten so angry. Now he wanted to know why she had changed her mind. "And when did this epiphany happen?"

"When I missed you," she said honestly.

And she had, missed him with an intensity that was almost frightening. With such an intensity that she had wanted to push him away. It didn't seem right that one human being should have such an effect on another. But she hadn't the strength to break away. She just wanted him in her life for as long as he wanted to remain.

Sheila gave in to her emotions. "Oh, God, Slade, I'm so scared. I'm a doctor and I know all the pluses, but I know the minuses, too. What if . . . ?"

He took her into his arms and held her tightly to him. He didn't want her to say it, didn't want to hear it. For both their sakes.

"There is no 'what if.' She's going to be fine. Just fine." He said the words fiercely, as if the sound could make it so.

Sheila pressed her lips together. She had to face the possibility. "Babies die."

He took her by the shoulders, holding her away from him, his eyes fixed on hers. She'd never seen them look so dark, so dangerous.

"Babies also live. A lot more of them do than don't. This isn't a Third World country, this is Southern California. And Harris Memorial is right up there among the best in the country. I know that. *You* know that."

She nodded, struggling to hold on to the fight within her. It felt as if it all had suddenly been drained off. "Intellectually."

His voice was harsh, demanding. He wasn't going to get anywhere by coddling her. He understood that. Coddling would make her fall apart. He wanted her strong.

"Well, slip the information to your emotional side." He nodded toward the cot. She needed rest more than she needed food. "And get some sleep."

She shook her head. Right now, she was overtired. "I don't think I can."

"Then I guess I'll just have to make you." Before she could ask how, Slade picked her up in his arms and carried her over to the first bed.

The last time she'd been in his arms this way felt like an eternity ago. Had that really been her, then? Had she ever felt light and carefree? She could barely remember.

"What are you doing?"

"Taking matters into my own hands." As gently as he could, he laid her down on top of the bed.

"This is for patients," she protested. She could feel her body crying out for rest. It was only her mind that refused to give in.

"Of which you will be one if you don't lie down before you drop," he insisted angrily. For a doctor, she had very little sense sometimes.

She had no energy with which to fight him. And the bed felt absolutely wonderful beneath her exhausted body. She felt as if she'd been up for days, but her mind was still on edge.

"It won't do any good," she protested. "I can't sleep."

"Then you'll lie there," Slade countered. The hell with the coffee. "And I'm going to sit right here to see that you do." He dragged the chair over to her bedside and positioned himself between Sheila and Rebecca's crib. He nodded toward the baby for her benefit. "See, she's asleep."

Sheila propped herself up on her elbow to get a better view of Rebecca. Soft lashes lay against her pink cheeks like tiny dark crescent moons. *She has to be all right, she just has to.* Sheila looked up at Slade. "She is, isn't she?"

"The injection they gave her is taking effect." He was just saying aloud what he knew Sheila was already aware of. "There's nothing for you to do but rest."

She laughed at his tone. "Hey, who's the doctor here?"

"You are." Sitting down in the chair, he leaned forward until his face was close to hers. "But I'm what the doctor ordered. Or at least I should be." He combed his fingers through her hair. "I've missed you, Sheila. Missed you a hell of a lot."

And she'd missed him. More than she ever knew was possible. "You didn't call."

Not because he hadn't wanted to. "I started to. Probably three or four dozen times."

And she had almost called his editor to ask where he'd been sent. But all she knew was the man's first name. It hadn't been much to go on, and her pride had prevented her from trying any further. And then Ingrid had become ill. And after that, Rebecca.

"None of the calls went through."

He nodded. "Because I thought you needed the time and the space to calm down. When I make a decision, it's one of those 'lightning striking' situations. I know what I want and I stick by it. You, on the other hand, need a little longer, so I decided to give it to you."

Slade took her hand in his, lacing his fingers through it. Binding himself to her.

"Now that we're here together, I just want you to know that I don't intend to get out of your life easily." He smiled at her. "Or ever. No matter what kind of arguments we'll have down the line—and we'll have them." She was as stubborn, as quick, with her tongue as he was. There was no way they weren't going to argue.

And make up. That would be the best part.

The smile left his face as he looked at her seriously. "You're what I want, Sheila, what I've always wanted." Even though, at the time, he hadn't known it. But that was why she had remained in his mind all those months, seductively whispering along the corners of his mind like a siren, calling him home. "A tall, beautiful woman with wit who just happens to be the mother of my baby." He pressed his lips to her hand.

"It doesn't hurt that each time I kiss you, the world tilts a little on its axis and my knees suddenly have the strength of a rubber chicken." He'd never said anything like that before, never felt anything like this before. And he knew he never would, not with any other woman. "We make magic together, Sheila. I know it, you know it. If I lied, it was because I was desperate."

Remembering, Slade stared out the window. Rain was still lightly bathing the panes, sliding down into tiny pools at the bottom.

He sighed. "I don't get desperate very often, but I did when I thought you weren't going to marry me. Standing there in the hospital, my baby minutes away from being born, I knew I wanted to make things right, for you, for the baby. And for me." He couldn't leave himself out of the equation. He was very much a part of it. "So I lied. I think I could be forgiven in a court of law. How about your court?"

He looked at Sheila when she didn't answer. But she had fallen asleep. Slowly disentangling his fingers, he laid her hand beside her.

"Some of my best rhetoric and you slept through it," he murmured, then grinned to himself. "I guess we really are married, after all."

Slade rose. Taking the blanket that was folded at the foot of the bed, he covered her. "Well, at least you finally listened to me."

He bent over Sheila and pressed a light kiss to her temple. Shifting slightly, she murmured something in her sleep, but didn't open her eyes.

He thought of what he had said to her. She needed to know how he felt. Which meant he had to say it all again when she was awake. "To be repeated in the morning."

Like a panther stalking prey in the forest, Slade moved his shoulders, trying to get rid of the ache he felt building right along his spine.

He knew it would dissipate once he knew that Rebecca was all right again.

"Is there anything that I can get for you, Mr. Garrett?"

Surprised to hear anyone in the room, Slade turned. There was a slender young nurse standing in the doorway, peering into the room. He thought of the coffee. He could use some right about now.

"Yeah, thanks. Coffee would be nice."

She nodded. There was a fresh pot on, not five minutes old. "How do you take it?"

"Thick and black."

"Like my husband," she noted with a smile. She was about to go and get it when she stopped, adding, "She's going to be all right. Your little girl, she'll be fine."

"Yeah." The answer was almost fierce, though quietly uttered. "I know."

She had to be.

Slade went to call Andy to tell him that he wouldn't be in tomorrow morning to polish the last installment of his story. Someone else could do that. Someone else could have the byline as well, if they wanted it. He didn't care about anything. Except the two people he left in the room behind him.

The coffee container he'd gotten from the nurse had long since become soggy and shapeless in his hand. When he'd finally drained the last of the dark liquid, it had become cold sludge. But it did what he wanted it to. It kept him awake.

Or, in some semblance of wakefulness, at any rate. He'd pulled up his chair directly beside the crib and kept vigil through the night, dozing in small, fitful increments. Nothing he hadn't done before a dozen times or more.

But this time it wasn't to wait out the break in an important story, or to interview a rebel leader holed up in the side of a mountain with his guerrilla followers. It was to wait out a fever, waiting for it to break. To know that he had his daughter back.

Because of her age, he knew just how serious the situation was. He'd encouraged Sheila, using all the right arguments at his disposal, but who was there to encourage him, he wondered.

Who did he lean on?

He glanced at Sheila as the sun's rays slowly slid into the room with them.

Her.

He could lean on her if he had to. They could be each other's strength. In Sheila he knew he'd found a soul mate for life. They had rough spots to iron out, but who didn't? That was what was going to keep it interesting. That, and the pulsating attraction that existed between them like a living entity.

He'd make it work. No, he amended, *they* would make it work.

With a deep sigh, he set down the stained cup on the floor and rose, stretching his cramped limbs. His mouth felt like dry cotton.

He wondered if there was any more coffee available. The nurse had been in an hour ago to check on Rebecca. She'd whispered to him, so as not to wake Sheila, that she was going off duty then. Someone named Kathy was coming on. Maybe he'd see if he could find her, he thought.

Slade looked down and saw that Rebecca was awake. She was lying in the crib, not making a sound.

Not crying.

She stared up at him with her bright blue eyes, watching every movement he made. And her eyes were clear. His heart leaped up in his chest. They were clear.

"Hey, good morning, Short Stuff," he whispered. "You gave your mom and me one heck of a scare last night." Very lightly, he ran his fingers along the silky cheek. It felt cool. "But you look a lot better now. I guess they're pumping you full of good things, huh?"

He never knew he could feel so grateful, so relieved. "Your eyes are clearer. I'm no doctor, of course, that's your mom's department. But I will be able to kiss your hurts away when you get them."

He leaned over the crib. Rebecca was looking at him as if she understood what he was saying. He got a kick out of the way her eyes seemed to follow every movement of his mouth.

"These lips are magic, did you know that? A lot of ladies have told me that. But that's all water under the bridge now since I met your mom. She's a pretty terrific lady, your mom. For that matter, I'm no slouch myself. You'll find that out soon enough for yourself."

Slade tucked the blanket around Rebecca. She moved her legs within the bunting she had on as if she was trying to kick them off. Probably didn't like the confinement, he guessed.

"You have to hurry up and get better so I can spring you out of here. There's a lot of things we're going to do together, you and me and your mom. I'm one of those progressive dads. I'm pleased as he—heck," he amended quickly. He was going to have to watch his language around her. "Pleased as heck that you're a girl. We're going to do all those things together men used to do with their sons. Play ball, go camping. I know how to make a lean-to out of leaves, ropes and ingenuity, kind of like MacGyver." He grinned at the thought. "And I can't wait to show you. Your mom and your two grandmothers can take care of the cultural end of the spectrum, but I'll show you what life's really all about."

He looked at his daughter, seeing her the way she would be in the years to come. He couldn't wait, he realized, and yet, part of him wanted to keep her the way she was for as long as possible.

"We're going to have a great life, Becky," he assured her. "Just the three of us. So you hurry up and lick that bug inside of you. Show it who's boss. You're a Garrett, and Garretts don't ever give up when they find something they want." She made a noise and he would have sworn on a stack of Bibles that she was agreeing with him. "And you're going to want this life we've got planned for you. There'll be some leeway and you'll have some input, but I promise you, you're going to love it."

His heart felt as if it was filled to the brim. "So hurry up and get better so we can take those tubes out of you, honey. Daddy wants to hold you again."

Slade stiffened when he felt the hand on his shoulder. He thought he was alone. Turning, he saw that Sheila was awake and standing beside him, her eyes bright with tears. They didn't say a word as they took each other into their arms.

"Welcome home," Sheila sobbed against his shoulder. "I forgot to say that last night."

"Thanks."

He didn't trust himself to say any more as he held her close, against his heart. Where she had been since the beginning.

Chapter Twelve

"Oh, Slade, she feels cooler. Touch her," Sheila urged.

It was the most unscientific of methods, but she knew. One touch to her daughter's forehead and Sheila just knew that Rebecca was getting better. Just as she had known that there was something wrong with her to begin with, before the fever had set in.

So this was motherhood, she thought, where instincts nudged their way ahead of tried-and-true professional training. Sheila smiled down at her baby.

Though he had done it just a few minutes ago, to please Sheila, Slade lay the back of his hand against the tiny forehead. In response, Rebecca squirmed. He knew she was too young to understand, but it looked as if she was trying to pull her arms free of the tethers that held them in place. She whimpered in what he was certain was the first signs of frustration.

Slade grinned at his daughter. He knew how that was.

"She does feel cooler. And her eyes are clear." He turned to Sheila and put his arm around her. They stood, just looking at their child, relieved beyond words. "See, I told you things were going to be all right."

"Sorry I doubted you," she quipped.

"Where do you want me to put them?"

They both turned around to see the morning shift nurse standing in the doorway.

"Them?" Sheila repeated. She exchanged looks with Slade. "Put what?"

"The flowers," the nurse explained, realizing she had gotten ahead of herself. "The nurses' station is completely inundated with floral arrangements." She gestured down the hall. "Come and see for yourself, Dr. Pollack."

Curious, Sheila and Slade followed the nurse into the hall.

"We don't normally place flowers in children's rooms. We keep them at the station and ask the parents to take them home when they arrive. But this is getting a little out of hand...."

The nurse let her voice trail off as she nodded toward the station. Sheila approached, staring at the colorful profusion in surprise. There were baskets, vases, bowls and animals made out of flowers placed on the center island where the records were kept as well as on every available flat surface.

"They're all ours?" Sheila asked incredulously.

A tall, thin nurse looked up from the center of the collection. She looked like a bee in a garden trying to decide which flower to land on first. "Every single last posy."

It looked like a florist shop had exploded. They'd only been here since a little before midnight. It was only past eight now. Sheila didn't understand where the flowers had come from.

"But from who?"

Slade picked up a card attached to the closest arrangement, a basket filled with daisies and with multicolored balloons tied to the handle. He read the message and grinned.

"This one's from Andy." He held the card up for her to see. "I guess he must have gotten the word out after I called him last night."

Sheila looked at Slade quizzically. When had he had time to make a call?

He read the question in her eyes. "I called him after you fell asleep. I told him I wouldn't be in the office this morning. I said to give the last of my installments to Kennedy to polish."

She had no idea who Kennedy was, but she would, she promised herself. She was going to get to know everyone who was a part of Slade's life. Part of her husband's life.

The thought brought a smile to her lips. Her husband. She figured she had about thirty or forty good years in which to do it.

Sheila plucked a card from the midst of an arrangement of carnations and baby's breath. "This one's from Marlene. How did she . . . ?" There was an explanation for how his editor had known to send flowers, but she hadn't called anyone about Rebecca. How had Marlene known to send flowers?

And then she glanced at the florist's name on top of the card and had her answer. "Erin."

Slade came up behind her, still holding his card. "Erin?" He had no idea who that was.

Sheila looked at the card. The logo across the top was the same. "These are from Erin's shop." She tapped the top of his card. " 'Flowers by Erin.' "

Slade read the address below the logo. The shop was located approximately three blocks from the hospital. "Andy must have called the closest florist to the hospital as soon as he was up."

"Which is Erin's." She'd used it herself on occasion and knew that Erin opened her shop at seven. "I delivered her baby on Valentine's Day," Sheila murmured, slipping the card back into its envelope.

She picked another card. Nicole and Dennis had sent a chrysanthemum arrangement shaped like a large yellow dog. It had daisies for eyes and a flower she didn't recognize for a nose. Sheila felt tears forming again. For a woman who didn't cry, she was getting entirely too weepy, she thought, taking the handkerchief that Slade offered.

"Erin must have gotten the word out to the others and they all sent flowers."

"Lots of others," Slade commented, looking at the abundance of flowers.

She'd read the rest of the cards later, Sheila thought. She laid her head against Slade's arm. It was nice to have the support of friends. And even better to have a man she was in love with to stand beside her. She began to understand what her parents had to be feeling these days, what they'd felt after her mother's test results had come in negative. This moment was the only one she had right here, right now, and it was up to her to make the most of it.

That meant not getting sidetracked by pride or anger. Or fear.

Slade drew out another card from a basket that seemed to contain every flower known to man. "Where are we going to put all these things?" The card was from the crew in the entertainment section.

"I can call Ingrid's sister. Her boyfriend has a van," she remembered.

Slade drew Sheila aside, away from the flowers and the nurses who were looking on and listening. They walked back to Rebecca's room. The baby was now sleeping peacefully. The sight gladdened his heart. "Rebecca's never dating anyone with a van."

Amusement nudged its way in, filling her for the first time since before Slade had left for his assignment. "Why, what did you do in vans?"

He grinned. "Things better not mentioned in mixed company." He'd just show her instead, he thought, as soon as she was able. As he shoved his hand into his pocket, his fingers came in contact with something. "Oh, I almost forgot. I brought you something from D.C."

She stared at him, not knowing what to expect.

Slade flipped open the small box in his pocket with his thumb, taking out the diamond-encrusted ring it held inside. He felt something stirring within him as he slipped the ring on her finger.

"Slade, it's beautiful," she whispered.

He shrugged. "Can't have a bride without a ring. Sorry it's late."

She shook her head. "No, it's right on time. And you don't have anything to be sorry about, not ever again."

He grinned. "I'll remind you of that from time to time."

"So, how's my patient doing?" Dr. Williams entered the room behind them. In a dapper suit and tie, he looked just slightly less formal than he had the night before.

"She's better, Ben."

He cast an appraising eye at Sheila. "I'm glad to hear that, but you look like hell, Sheila."

She combed her hand through her hair. She could use a good shower and some clean clothes. A toothbrush wouldn't have hurt, either. But none of it mattered. Rebecca's fever had broken and that lit up her soul like a Fourth of July exhibition.

She grinned at the older man. "Is that your medical opinion?"

Dr. Williams looked at her, his expression as stern as when he was lecturing one of his own daughters. Picking up Rebecca's chart, he quickly skimmed the notations.

"That's my observation as a human being." He glanced at Slade as he laid the chart aside. "Can't you get your wife to go home and take a nap, change her clothes, take a shower?" Quickly, competently, he examined Rebecca. "Make herself presentable?"

"No, no, no, and she already is." He watched the doctor listen to Rebecca's heart and lungs. "Sheila's a very independent lady."

The doctor snorted as he draped the stethoscope around the back of his neck. "Well, my condolences to you, then. You've got your hands full. I know. I married one of those independent women." He looked at Rebecca with a smile. "They raise independent daughters."

Slade didn't care how dependent they were, as long as they were well. "So, what's the verdict?"

"Prognosis," Sheila corrected him automatically. Her eyes were trained on the doctor's face. She'd watched every movement, looking for a sign that would alert her that things were not as good as they seemed. There weren't any. Still, she wasn't the type to immediately ignore the negative. "What *is* the prognosis, Ben?"

The doctor smiled. "Very favorable." Nothing gave him more pleasure than to pronounce one of the children on the road to recovery. "She's doing a lot better than some of my other patients." He took out the chart again to record his findings. "Must be that iron constitution she's inherited from you. She's retaining more fluid." He paused to consider. "I'd say that she'll probably be ready to go home tomorrow."

The news was good, very good. But she had wanted more. "Not today?"

He understood her eagerness. He'd feel the same in her shoes. Had felt the same. "Not today, Sheila. We're a cautious hospital, remember? But it looks as if the crisis has passed. Wonderful resilience, babies. They never cease to amaze me." After making one final note on the chart, he flipped it closed and handed it to the nurse at his side to put away. "Want a little advice? As a father of three, not your daughter's pediatrician."

Slade draped his arm around Sheila's shoulders, answering before she did. "Yes?"

"Utilize this time. She's mending, we're taking great care of her." Nothing worse than parents underfoot, even parents with medical degrees. Especially parents with medical degrees, he amended, remembering himself when his oldest had come down with meningitis. "Go home and get some sleep." He smiled as he looked at Rebecca. "It might be the last chance you have to get more than three hours at a time for months. My first one didn't sleep through the night until she was four."

"Months?" Slade asked incredulously.

"Years," Dr. Williams clarified. "Go home, both of you. I'll be here to discharge her tomorrow."

Pleased with himself and with the progress he saw in this room, Dr. Williams left to see to his other patients on the floor.

The relief in the small room was almost palpable. Slade let out a huge breath he hadn't been aware he was holding. Sliding his hands into his pockets, he looked at Sheila.

"So, what do you say?" he asked. "Do you want to go home for a few hours?" He could really stretch out on a bed now, he thought. Now that Rebecca was out of danger. Now that his marriage was back on track.

Sheila felt completely energized by Williams's prognosis. With worry stripped from her, she felt like a butterfly freed of the confines of a dark, oppressive cocoon. Looking down at her wedding ring, she shook her head. "No, I want to go sightseeing."

"Sightseeing?" he echoed. That would have been the last thing he would have thought she'd want—if it would have occurred to him at all. "Sure you're feeling all right?"

He laid the back of his hand across her forehead, just as he had across Rebecca's. It was cool. So why was she talking crazy?

"I'm feeling just fine," Sheila assured him.

The mischief in her eyes gave him his first inkling. They'd looked that way the night of the party. The night his destiny had been changed forever. "Just what did you have in mind?"

She splayed her hand along his chest as she looked up at him, her body teasing his. "There's this certain little cove I'm partial to. It's located on a private beach. The owners are away again on another one of their endless cruises." She could never understand going away on an expensive cruise when the ocean was practically knocking at your door. "I thought I might want to see it again." Her smile was seductive. "It isn't far from here."

His arm tightened around hers. Desire, hidden these last hours, rose full-blooded in his veins. "I remember. It might look different in the light."

"No, it won't." She shook her head, the last of her hair coming undone, brushing along his shoulder. "Because you'll be there with me."

All the rest of my days, Sheila. All the rest of my days. "Does this mean I can unpack?"

He already knew the answer to that, she thought. She never really wanted him to leave. Not if she examined her heart.

"As fast as you can—but later. I really want to see that cove now." Her head tilted up; her mouth was just inches away from his. "It's pretty isolated this time of year, you know."

He could see himself making love with her. Feel himself making love with her. "Don't tempt me."

She laughed. "I intend to, Slade Garrett. I intend to do just that all the days of your life."

She meant it, he thought. She really meant it. "Sounds like exquisite torture to me."

"Good." She kissed him soundly, opening the door a crack to what there was waiting for him. For them. Her breath was just the slightest bit shaky as she added, "Because you're in for a lot of it."

If she thought that was a threat, she was going to be disappointed with its effect. "Promises, promises..."

He took her hand, drawing her out of the room. They had a great deal of catching up to do, unencumbered by doubts or fears or hurt feelings.

"Wait," one of the nurses called after them as they began walking toward the elevators. "What about the flowers?"

Instead of answering, Slade retraced his steps to the nurses' station. Sheila followed, curious. She watched as Slade took a daisy from one of the arrangements. He slid the stem into her hair, the way he had tucked the flower behind her ear the night they met. Then it had come from one of the centerpieces at the banquet. Now it came from a get-well basket intended for their daughter.

"There, perfect," he murmured. "Take the cards out of the arrangements for us," he told the nurse. "And then distribute the flowers to some of the other patients who don't have any." He raised his brow to see if Sheila agreed.

"My thoughts exactly." She smiled. "We think alike, Slade."

Yes, on the fundamental things, they did. And always would. "That means you know what I'm thinking."

Her grin was wide. "Yes, I do." She laced her hand through his. "Let's go," she whispered.

He hesitated just a moment. "Can you?"

"I can." It had been more than two weeks, and she knew her own body. She was ready, willing and able. "C'mon, we're wasting time."

"Not anymore, Sheila," he said as they hurried to the elevator. "Not anymore."

*   *   *   *   *

You've read **Do You Take This Child?**

Now, don't you want more great stories from

Well, we've got 'em!

In May 1996, discover what happens when a child's entry in a Mother's Day contest puts lonely-hearts expert and single mom Rosemary Gallagher in the unwitting position of making a date…for herself!

Join the fun in LET'S GET MOMMY MARRIED,
RITA-Award-winning author
Marie Ferrarella's newest title, found only in—

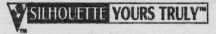

Love—when you least expect it!

They're the hardest working, sexiest women in the Lone Star State...they're

Annette Broadrick

The O'Brien sisters: Megan, Mollie and Maribeth. Meet them and the men who want to capture their hearts in these titles from Annette Broadrick:

MEGAN'S MARRIAGE
(February, Silhouette Desire #979)

The *MAN OF THE MONTH* is getting married to *very* reluctant bride Megan O'Brien!

INSTANT MOMMY
(March, Silhouette Romance #1139)

A *BUNDLE OF JOY* brings Mollie O'Brien together with the man she's always loved.

THE GROOM, I PRESUME?
(April, Silhouette Desire #992)

Maribeth O'Brien's been left at the altar—but this bride won't have to wait long for wedding bells to ring!

Don't miss the DAUGHTERS OF TEXAS—three brides waiting to lasso the hearts of their very own cowboys! Only from

 and ▼ *Silhouette* ROMANCE™

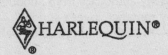

"Motherhood is full of love, laughter
and sweet surprises. Silhouette's collection
is every bit as much fun!"
—Bestselling author **Ann Major**

This May, treat yourself to...

WANTED:
MOTHER

Silhouette's annual tribute to motherhood takes a
new twist in '96 as three sexy single men prepare for
fatherhood—and saying "I Do!" This collection makes
the perfect gift, not just for moms but for all romance
fiction lovers! Written by these captivating authors:

Annette Broadrick
Ginna Gray
Raye Morgan

"The Mother's Day anthology from Silhouette is the
highlight of any romance lover's spring!"
—Award-winning author **Dallas Schulze**

MD96